THE MERMAID GIRL

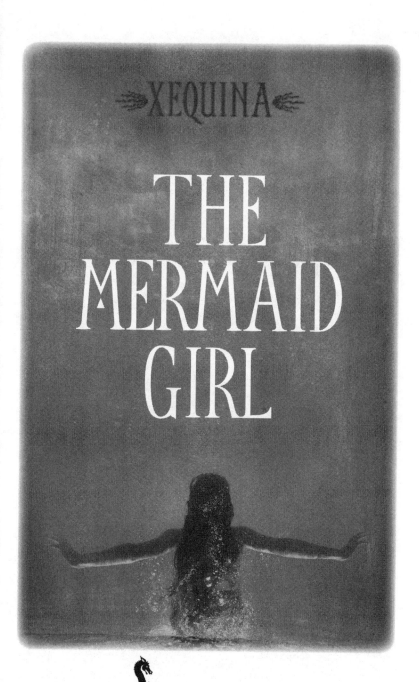

THE MERMAID GIRL

≈XEQUINA≈

Dragonfeather Books
Bedazzled Ink Publishing Company • Fairfield, California

978-1-943837-56-4 paperback
978-1-943837-57-1 epub
978-1-943837-67-0 mobi

Cover Design
by

DESIGNS

Dragonfeather Books
a division of
Bedazzled Ink Publishing, LLC
Fairfield, California
http://www.bedazzledink.com

To Mermaid Girls everywhere

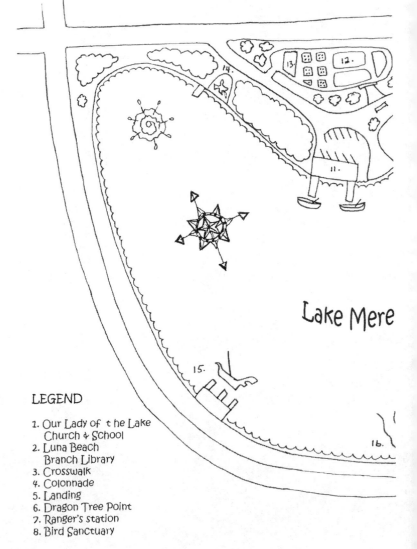

Lake Mere

LEGEND

1. Our Lady of the Lake
   Church & School
2. Luna Beach
   Branch Library
3. Crosswalk
4. Colonnade
5. Landing
6. Dragon Tree Point
7. Ranger's station
8. Bird Sanctuary

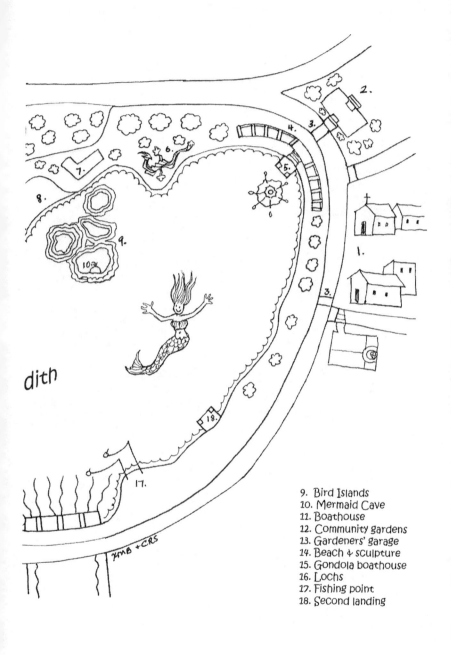

dith

CHAPTER 1
A MOST AMAZING DISCOVERY

The day I found the mermaid it had been raining hard. The huge storms that caused some flooding were over. They weren't bad enough to make us evacuate Luna Beach, but there was damage and everyone stayed away from the shore. The giant waves could sweep people and even cars into the sea.

I liked the storms. I loved looking at the rain from my bedroom window; hearing the howling wind and watching the enormous waves crash onto the beach and promenade. I got to wear my rubber boots every day. They were lime green with orange frogs and handles on the rims to pull them on. There were big pools of water, and sometimes I found shells and water-polished rocks, and once a little fish. I wanted to keep it but my mother wouldn't let me.

"It's a baby leopard shark," she told me. "It'll grow too big, and anyway, it's wild and needs to live in the ocean." She helped me catch it in a bucket, and then we carried it to the beach to set it free. I was sad, but my mother's a marine biologist, so she knows what's best for sea life.

We lived about a block away from the beach. At the lowest corner of our house was an open drain with a basin about four feet long and two feet wide to catch rainwater from the gutters. It was overflowing now, because the drain was clogged with mud and leaves. One day after school I stopped to look into it. There was something swimming around, long and thin, and looked like a greenish earthworm, but it had mossy seaweed on its head, and a couple of projections that it was using to swim.

I crouched down to get a better look. It swam away, down to the bottom, where it hid in a pale green eggshell. There were two halves, not quite broken apart, and the worm-creature was curled up inside it. When I picked it up, the creature wiggled out of the shell and dove back into the water, where it hid in the mud.

I couldn't believe what I'd seen. It looked like a tiny mermaid!

The shell was smaller than a hen's egg, and the color reminded me of light seen in a swimming pool, when you opened your eyes underwater. I put the shell back in the water and waited to see if the mermaid would come out again. She was moving, like she was trying to nestle down further into the mud.

"Camile!" my mother called. "Where are you, honey?"

After another long look, I picked up my books and went inside.

CHAPTER 2
MY MOTHER

My mother was working at the computer. "I noticed you outside. Were you playing?"

I nodded. I put my knapsack and lunch box down. I was too surprised to say anything about what I'd found. Anyway, I wasn't really sure it was a mermaid I'd seen. My mother had told me they were a legend.

Her thick black hair was in a ponytail to keep it out of her eyes when she works, and she still had on the old clothes she wears because her job is messy. She works at a research lab and preserve down the coast from Luna Beach. She observes the animals and nurses sick and injured ones. She also tests water in the different tanks, prepares the animals' food, and helps to clean up after them. Sometimes she dissects and studies dead animals. At home she works on grants to keep the preserve funded.

"How was school today? What did you learn?"

I had to think hard because I was really distracted. "We practiced writing." I stared out the window. Was that really a mermaid?

"Cammie? Honey? Are you listening to me?"

I turned back to my mother.

"I asked what you wrote about."

"Oh. Pets."

"Pets?"

"Amigo."

Amigo was the neighbor's cat. We didn't have any pets. My parents said I had to wait until I was older and could be responsible for one. I knew it was because my mother takes care of animals at work and didn't want to end up doing it at home too.

"Would you read me what you wrote?"

What I really wanted to do was go look for the mermaid. "Later?" I asked. "Can I play for a while?"

My mother looked out the window. "All right, but come back in if it starts raining."

I made sure she was back at work before I went out. I ran up to the basin of the drain and saw a disturbance of surface water like a fish made when they were scared. All I could see was a trace of mud floating up through the water, where the creature had gone back to hide. I found a stick and stirred the mud, but she wouldn't come out. I stayed until my mother called me to come in. I still didn't tell my mother what I'd seen.

"Mom, what would you do if you found a mermaid?" I asked during dinner.

"Mermaids aren't real, Camile."

"But . . . what if they *were* real, and you found one?"

"Well, that would be a really important discovery, since no mermaid has ever been found. I'd take her to the research lab where she could be studied. First we'd make sure the environment was right for her, and find out what foods she ate. We wouldn't want to add to the stress of being captured by giving her the wrong food. When an organism is under stress, it's difficult to study DNA expression and biochemistry."

"Does being put into captivity cause stress?"

"Yes, because it would be a drastic change from what she's used to. Change always creates stress. And when any animal is under stress, their body's biochemistry changes, so the way they respond to food and environment will be different. Want more salad?" She gave us both more carrot salad.

"What would you do next?"

"We'd take samples to study under a microscope, and X-rays of her whole body, so we would probably put her under sedation so she wouldn't know what was happening."

"But wouldn't that be dangerous?"

"Yes, but we have very safe methods, and so far, we haven't lost too many animals that way."

Not too many—which meant they *had* lost some.

"We would perform lots of experiments with her, because the more we do, the more we can learn about mermaids. If she could talk, we'd bring in linguistics experts to study sound patterns and learn her language, so we could talk to other mermaids when we found them. We'd also teach her to speak English. Then we'd be able to ask her questions, and trust me, we'd have thousands. I'm sure the scientists who work with dolphin and human communication would want to work with her as well.

"She would probably be sent to a bigger research lab so she could be studied more in depth. They have a lot more instruments they could use for testing. A facility would probably be built specially for her with one-way mirrors, microphones, and video cameras. Also, scientists from all over the world would want to come to see her, and they would have their own studies and experiments to conduct."

"When everyone was done with their tests and questions, would you set the mermaid free?"

My mother thought about it. "I suppose we could; then we could put a little camera on her so we could monitor where she goes and what she does, and a tracking device so we could find out where other mermaids lived. We'd learn even more about her that way. But I think she'd be too important a discovery to just turn loose again. Most likely we would try to find and catch more mermaids instead."

They would make a complete prisoner out of her. It all sounded like a tiring and awful way to be forced to live. I couldn't imagine them putting that tiny creature through all of that, and her surviving. And what about privacy? She would never have any again. I decided not to tell my mother what I'd found.

CHAPTER 3
FEEDING A MERMAID

When I got home from school the next day I went back to the open drain, walking slowly and staying as far as I could to see if the creature-thing was out. Sure enough, she was swimming lazily around the basin. I got a good look. I hadn't been seeing things. The upper part of her body was like a person, with a little head and arms, long, wispy, dark green hair like fine seaweed, and tiny bluish fins on her forearms and down the middle of her back. Her lower body looked like an earthworm, only without the rings along the length. Her skin looked like delicate human skin, except it was pale green.

I edged closer. Immediately the mermaid dove and hid under a rock. I was disappointed because I'd scared her again. I walked around the basin and looked into the water from all sides, but couldn't see anything. I waited a long time, but the mermaid didn't come out.

While I sat there, I looked at the water. The bottom had mud and some old leaves, and there were a few rocks with moss growing on them. There were also a few soggy worms. I started fishing them out with the stick to put them on the grass, then wondered if that was the mermaid's food. What did she eat? And did she have enough food?

I started wondering what mermaids ate. They came from the ocean, so it had to be fish or seaweed, or both. I went inside.

My mother wasn't home from work yet. I opened a can of tuna and took out a pinch, then looked in the refrigerator. I tore off a small piece of lettuce. I also took a little bit of bread. Since goldfish and carp ate bread, maybe mermaids did too.

I took them out to the basin and sprinkled them on top of the water, then backed away to watch from a distance.

The bread and lettuce floated for a while, but the tuna sank. Suddenly the mermaid darted up, out from the mud and grabbed some in her tiny hands and ate it. I noticed she had only three fingers and a thumb, with webs between them. After the mermaid ate, she swam over to investigate the bread and lettuce, which were now slowly drifting through the water. She nibbled at them.

It was so interesting to watch the mermaid that I didn't even realize I was moving closer. The next thing I knew I was leaning over the water and the mermaid saw me and quickly disappeared again.

After that I brought the mermaid something every day, different foods like apple, hamburger, raw and cooked, the tender stalk of green onion, zucchini, or tomato. Once, when my dad came home with a big platter of sushi, I was able to give the mermaid raw fish, grains of rice, and even some seaweed, all of which she seemed to love. There were also things she didn't like, onions and hot peppers, although she ate sweet red pepper. In this way, I learned that mermaids are omnivorous. That means they eat just about everything, like humans.

CHAPTER 4
PATIENCE

That Saturday I sat near the pool, waiting to see if the mermaid would come out. I was watching the water so carefully that I didn't noticed my mother coming toward me.

"What are you looking at, Camile?"

I jumped, then tried to think of what to say. Finally I just said, "Tadpoles."

"Did you find any?" She crouched down next to me to look into the water.

I picked up the stick and I stirred up the water because it scared the mermaid, and I didn't want her to come out right then.

"Just worms. I put them on the lawn."

"That was very kind of you. Without earthworms, the ground would be a dead, dry place." She sat there for a while, looking into the water too, turning her head so she could see around the sides of the rocks. I was worried she would see the mermaid squirming in the mud the way she did sometimes and wonder what it was. Finally my mother got up.

"I have to go to the grocery store. Want to come along?"

I really wanted to keep watch for the mermaid, but I didn't want my mother to suspect something really amazing was living in the open drain, so I went with her.

On the way to the store I asked, "Mom, what happens when animals at the center are afraid of you?"

"I just have to wait until they learn to trust me."

"Does it take long?"

"Yes, because their first instinct is to stay away from humans. Remember, most species have learned over the ages that humans and a lot of other animals are very dangerous and would try to kill and eat them. So you learn to wait, and show them over time that you're not going to hurt them. Patience is probably the most important skill you learn, doing this kind of work."

Of course I already knew the mermaid had the same instinct

to avoid me. But just by watching the mermaid, I was learning an important scientific skill.

After that, I sat on the side of the basin where I could keep an eye on the house so I would know if someone was coming toward me. And whenever my mom or dad called me, I went right away no matter what was happening with the mermaid. I didn't want them to come looking for me and find out about the mermaid by accident.

CHAPTER 5
SCHOOL AND LIBRARY

I go to Our Lady of the Lake school. It's a parish school next to the church we go to, about a half mile from where we live. The church and school are across the street from Lake Meredith. I wear a uniform to school with a blue plaid skirt, white Peter Pan blouse, dark blue jacket, and black-and-white saddle shoes. I take my lunch to school in a Hello Kitty lunch box.

I'm really shy and don't talk. I never raise my hand in class. If the teacher calls on me I'll answer, I'm just really quiet. The good news is that I never get in trouble for talking, the way some kids do.

But there's a big down side to not talking. For one, I didn't have any friends. Also, I was always the last one to get picked for kickball and baseball, and I wasn't invited at all for smaller games. Worse than that, I didn't get invited places. I usually found out about parties because I heard girls talking about what they did, and how much fun it was. Like this week, they were talking about a slumber party.

"Wasn't that movie good?"

"Yes, especially the part where you first see the zombies."

"I can't believe we got to stay up until after midnight."

"And then we got blueberry pancakes in the morning!"

I tried not to mind. Part of the problem was I didn't know what to talk about. Even at home I didn't say very much. I heard my parents talking about it when they didn't realize I was listening (one good thing about being quiet—all the things I find out).

My mom said, "Her teachers tell me she doesn't speak up in class or talk to the other students."

"She talks to us," my dad said.

"Usually not unless we talk to her. What if it's some kind of disorder?"

"Inez, she was evaluated by the school nurse. If she thought there was a problem, she would have recommended further tests." They talked about it some more, until my dad said, "Don't pathologize the issue. I'm sure she'll grow out of it."

I snuck away to look up "pathologize." It means to treat something about a person as if it was abnormal. I guess it *was* a little abnormal not being able to talk to people. No one else seemed to have that problem.

That week our class went to the library. We go every three weeks to return books and get new ones. The library is near our school, so we don't have to walk very far. We gathered in a big room with tall windows and lots of chairs where we met the new children's librarian, Ms. Tanglewood. She talked about how she was looking forward to helping us find books and articles for our school work.

"Your teacher will let me know ahead of time what subjects you're studying, and I'll make sure to have lots of books on that topic for you to use or check out. And if you're interested in a particular subject, ask me and I'll find materials for you.

"And don't forget the study center is here for your use. You can come here after school to use the computers, do homework, or meet classmates and study together," Ms. Tanglewood said. "And of course, get help from me."

After that we went into the main part of the library. The shelves were crowded with books and the walls had lots of colorful art work and posters with famous people saying, "Read!" On one end of the room were a couple of large tables and several computers, which was the homework center.

Some kids sat down to use the computers. The rest of us wandered around, looking at books and showing them to each other. No one showed me any books, although my teacher found a book on Hispanic women from history she thought I might like. I found a book about angels and another about the ocean. When Ms. Tanglewood wasn't busy, I gave her a note asking for books on mermaids. She went to the computer and did a search. A printer came on and some pages came out.

"The library system has ninety-nine titles on mermaids." She found the first one on the list for me. It was a large picture book of mermaid stories with beautiful drawings.

I sat down, excited, and started reading. I didn't even realize our visit was over and we were supposed to be lining up to head back to school. My teacher, Mrs. Padma, had to come and get me.

I read the book all through the lunch hour and was still looking at it during class, so Mrs. Padma took it away from me.

"Now is not the time to read. You should be paying attention to the lesson," she reprimanded.

I was embarrassed because I *had* been paying attention. I was only looking at the pictures, but I folded my hands and kept my eyes on Mrs. Padma. She gave the book back before I went home that day.

CHAPTER 6
A HOUSE FOR A MERMAID

I usually walked home after school because my mom has odd hours, so I always stopped by the open drain before going inside. The mermaid wasn't as afraid anymore since I started feeding her, plus I was making progress. She used to hide again after she ate, but now she stayed out and I could watch her. It was really hard not to reach a finger out to her, but I made myself sit still and just look.

Today she was out swimming around so I showed her the mermaid book. It had beautiful mermaids on the cover with flowing hair, but after glancing at it for a moment, she didn't seem very interested. So I went inside and put my things down and changed before going back outside. I was allowed to play before dinner and I always spent that time watching the mermaid.

Sometimes the mermaid swam like I did in the summer, using her arms and doing side strokes, but she could also swim just by leading with her head and waggling her long body like a snake, her long, mossy hair trailing behind her. I noticed the skin of her tail was changing; it looked less like skin, glistening slightly with iridescence. She was growing.

"Mermary," I said all of a sudden, and she looked up. I don't know what made me think of it, but I thought it was a good name.

She swam through a branch from a tree that I found one day and put in her water. It was almost white, all the bark had fallen off. I realized Mermary didn't really have any shelter except for those rocks and the mud at the bottom where she was always hiding. The book showed mermaids living in sea caves or sunken ships or a giant clamshell. What could I find for her to live in? I thought about balancing a flat rock over two other rocks, but what if it fell on her? Then I thought about a bottle, but was afraid someone might see it and recycle it with Mermary in it. I was still thinking about it when I saw my mother's car turning down the block. It was time to leave the mermaid and go inside.

That evening as I was getting ready for bed, I picked up the orange helmet shell I had on my dresser. It had belonged to my grandmother, who had died. It was brown and a pretty peachy-orange color, with raised ridges and bumpy areas of white. On the back was carved the head of a lady with flowers in her long, wavy hair. When I was little, my grandmother told me the carving was called a cameo, and that it was the portrait of a little lady who used to live inside the shell. The inside was pearly smooth, and of course, it sounded like the ocean when I put it up to my ear. I thought it might make a nice house for the mermaid.

The next day I took it outside and put it into Mermary's pool. She immediately swam over to it and swam around and around it, running her tiny hands over the carving and rubbing up against the natural bumps and ridges on the outside like a cat does with furniture. Finally she followed the smooth mouth of the shell and slipped inside. After a moment she came back out and looked up at me. It seemed like she was smiling!

I put rocks around the shell so it wouldn't be so obvious it was there, in case someone passed by. Now Mermary had a perfect little mermaid house.

CHAPTER 7
BOOKS AND MOVIES ABOUT MERMAIDS

Some days I went to the library after school, usually when my mother could pick me up. I had started from the top of Mrs. Tanglewood's list and crossed off titles after reading them. But sometimes I couldn't find one. I finally showed her the list with the missing ones circled.

"Sometimes items might be checked out. Or they're materials owned by other libraries in the system," she explained. "I can order them for you."

Some were books of fairy tales, some were mythology. A couple were whole books of mermaid stories. A lot I thought of as baby books that were simple or silly and were for small children, but most had nice, colorful pictures and I read them anyway.

Ms. Tanglewood showed me how to use the online resources on the children's computer. There was a Children's Encyclopedia where I looked up mermaids. It said they were a "fable," which is a type of legendary story. There was also a thesaurus, which helps you find words of the same meaning. I looked up "mermaid" and found all the different names they're called: sirens, water nymphs, nixies, naiads, simbi, and sea maids. In Ireland they were called merrows, in Mexico sirenas, and in Russia, rusalkas. Another dictionary called them "monsters." Mermary was *not* a monster.

There was a lot of information on Wikipedia, but I knew I wasn't supposed to trust everything it said. Mrs. Padma said it was unreliable, and there was a school rule that we couldn't use it for our reports. It said Christopher Columbus had seen mermaids while he was exploring the Caribbean, and that there had been sightings of mermaids in countries around the world, even in the twentieth and twenty-first centuries.

There were a lot of mermaid movies on the list too. Some I'd already seen, like Disney's *Little Mermaid* and Barbie's *Mermaidia*. Some movies had mermaids in them, like *Hook*. I loved watching the mermaid scenes. Some looked so real I wondered if the film makers had found real mermaids to put in their movies.

What I thought was that mermaids probably co-existed with humans a long time ago, and that was why there were so many stories about them. But maybe humans drove them close to extinction, like we have lots of other animals, and the survivors learned to stay far away from humans.

One movie I saw was *Splash*, from the eighties, and I watched it with my mother. It's about a beautiful mermaid who falls in love with a guy named Allen after she saves him from drowning. Her tail changes into legs when she goes on land, so no one can tell she's really a mermaid. She finds him and they have a great time and fall in love. When people find out she's a mermaid, government men grab her and put her in a tank in a secret basement laboratory where they perform experiments. The mermaid curls up at the bottom of the tank and starts wasting away. The scientist who revealed her secret is worried about her condition, but the head scientist doesn't care and starts making plans to dissect her when she's dead. That really scared me and I started crying. I just knew the same thing would happen to my little mermaid if they knew I had her.

"Don't cry," my mother said. "You know mermaids aren't real."

"But what if they are?" I asked. "What if someday, a real mermaid is discovered? They would put her in a laboratory to study her, just like in the movie."

My mother sighed and said, "Well, that's how we learn about nature."

She said that like it was okay, but it wasn't. She was a marine scientist, exactly the kind of scientist who would want to study Mermary. How would scientists like it if mermaids caught them, and put them in a cage and gave them a bunch of boring tests to see how smart they were? Or worse, force them to do silly tricks for food? People had rights; didn't mermaids?

I knew it was only a matter of time before humans captured a mermaid to study, but I couldn't let it be Mermary. I couldn't tell anyone about her, ever.

CHAPTER 8
A SONG FOR A MERMAID

It seemed like the mermaid started to be interested in me. She came out every day to see if I'd brought her anything, but after looking at me for a minute or so, she'd go back to swimming. I wished I could have more interaction with her. I had already learned Mermary was afraid when I stirred the water with the stick, so I didn't use it anymore and just tried to be patient.

All the storm rain caused the trees and flowers to bloom, and one day I brought Mermary some blossoms I collected. When I sprinkled them on the water, the mermaid ate some of the petals, then played with them. It was fun to watch.

That weekend was warm. I took a walk and gathered some flowers and put them in the water for Mermary. As I sat there watching her, I started humming. The mermaid looked up.

Could she hear through the water? I hummed louder and the mermaid swam closer to me, so then I stopped humming to see if it made a difference. She waited, then went back to the flowers.

I wondered what Mermary would do if I sang a song. This was the kind of thing my mother did at her work, try experiments to see how the animals would react. When I was in the first grade we learned a mermaid song, "The Blue Mermaid." I started singing it.

The mermaid swam back to me, and this time, put her head out of the water. Even after I was finished, Mermary kept looking at me, so I sang it again. To my amazement, she started singing too! Not the words, she just sang "o-o-o-o-o" to the melody, and her voice was so pretty! She even sang while she was swimming on top of the water. At first it was the Blue Mermaid tune, then she started changing it.

Every day after that I sang to her first thing, and she always sang with me. If I learned a song in school that day, I would sing it for her. "Puff the Magic Dragon" was one of my favorites. One time after singing that song, I talked about what it meant, about the little boy Jackie growing up and leaving behind his toys. It seemed like Mermary was listening to me.

That's how I started talking to the mermaid. I'd tell her what I did in school that day. I told her about my teacher and classmates. I told her about my mom and dad, and what they did at work. I started thinking about other things to tell her, like if something fun happened at school. And now when I gave Mermary food, I told her what it was, and how it grew, like "apricots grow on trees. That's a tree," and I would point to a nearby tree that she could see. Mermary would look at me with her big green eyes and look at where I was pointing, so we were communicating in a way.

Mermary's mother probably would have taught her to talk if she hadn't gotten separated from her. I wondered about her mother. What had happened to her? Had the storms separated them? Did Mermary have brothers and sisters?

"I wish you could talk," I told Mermary.

She looked up and smiled.

CHAPTER 9
CONVERSATION

The next day, I went out to see the mermaid and I said hello. Mermary came up to the surface and put her head out of the water.

"Hello," she said back.

I was so amazed, I couldn't say anything at first.

"How are you?" I asked, when I got over my shock.

The mermaid seemed to think. "I'm wet," she said.

I laughed and clapped my hands. "You can talk!"

She clapped too. "I learned by listening to you. I didn't know I could talk until I tried."

So I started asking her lots of questions, like if she was cold in the pool and did she like living in the drain's basin, and the shell. I realized that was exactly what my mother said scientists would do, so after the first time, I tried not to ask so many at one time. I didn't want to tire her out.

After that we talked every day, and we'd always sing songs together. I asked if she had been born in the shell she was hiding in that first day, but she didn't know. By now the shell had disintegrated.

"All I remember is that I was in this pond, and then one day you came. You were so big, I was scared."

Mermary asked a lot of questions too.

"Are there others like me?"

"There must be," I said. "That's the only explanation of how you came to be."

"Where are they?"

"I don't know, they must be in the ocean because they're definitely not in lakes or rivers, like they probably were at one time."

Mermary also asked about her own environment, like where water from the sky comes from, or what the sun was. One day she told me, "An animal came and drank out of my pool. It had big eyes and pointy ears on top of its head. It was black and white and furry. What was that?"

"That's the neighbor's cat, Amigo," I told her. "He's a nice cat with people, but you're not safe around him. Cats like to eat fish and catch small animals. When you see him, swim to the bottom of the basin and stay there until he goes away."

Now that Mermary and I could converse together, I taught her the alphabet and numbers and the colors, and the names of the parts of her body and mine. I told her about the books I was reading, and now when I showed them too her, she was interested. Mermary was very curious, and I was giving her an education.

CHAPTER 10
MERMAID FACTS

At school we were learning about the different classes of animals: fish, birds, mammals, reptiles, and amphibians. Mammals are warm-blooded and nurse their young. Reptiles are cold-blooded, have scales, and usually lay eggs. Fish are cold-blooded, have gills and scales, and live in water. Amphibians are also cold blooded. They're born from eggs, and start the first part of their life with gills and living in water. Then they develop lungs and legs and live both in water and on land.

This made me wonder what class mermaids were in. They weren't a fish, but they weren't amphibians either. Mermary had gills, but she also breathed air. Furthermore, Mermary might have come from an egg. When I couldn't figure it out on my own, I waited until school was over for the day and handed a note to my teacher. I had written,

What class are mermaids in?

Mrs. Padma read the note and smiled. "They would be mammals that live in the ocean, like seals or dolphins. We know that because they have breasts and nurse their young."

I thought about that as I walked home, but I didn't think that was exactly right either. Sea mammals have hair, and don't have scales. But Mermary had hair and maybe scales on her fish-part, because it looked iridescent, although she was still too tiny to tell. And then there was the eggshell, although that could have been blown into the basin from a nearby nest.

So then I asked my mother if there were any sea animals that had hair and scales.

"No. Animals with hair are in a different evolutionary class than animals with scales."

I decided that mermaids must be in a class of their own, which of course hadn't been discovered because scientists hadn't found a mermaid yet.

My father was home that weekend. He was a physicist and was currently doing research in Europe. I went to the office supply store with him. While I was wandering around I found a stand of notebooks on sale. They were colorful and hardly any two were the same. I found a turquoise-green book with drawings of mermaids on the cover, and that gave me an idea. My mother kept notebooks about the animals they had in the research center so she could see their progress. I decided to do the same with Mermary. I had my own money from my allowance, so I bought it, along with a pen with bright green ink that smelled like limeade.

That night in bed, with the green pen and mermaid notebook, I started writing down what I knew about Mermary so far:

> Mermary might have been born from an egg.
> Mermaids can live in fresh water, but they can live
> in brackish water too.

Brackish water is fresh water that mixes with sea water, like at the area where a river pours into the ocean. I knew this because I tasted the water in the basin when I first discovered the mermaid. It was salty from the storms, but not as salty as the ocean. Then, when the water in the basin started going down from evaporation, I added water with the hose, and Mermary liked it.

> Mermaids are omnivorous.
> Mermaids can sing.
> Mermaids can talk.

> Mermaids are curious.
> Mermaids are intelligent.
> Mermaids have three fingers and a thumb.
> Mermaids have webbed fingers.
> Mermaids have gills and can stay underwater for
> a long time.

Most of what I was learning about Mermary would be from observation, like my mother did at her job. Now I understood why people studied animals and had to observe them over long periods of time. I thought about scientists observing a mermaid if they ever caught one. Once they realized mermaids could talk, they probably wouldn't be patient, but get right into questioning her and making her take intelligence tests. I hated that idea.

I wondered why mermaids hadn't been found yet. Was it because they were extremely good about hiding? Mermary's coloring made it hard for me to see her in the drain basin sometimes, so maybe it was mermaids' protective coloring that has kept them from being discovered. I wrote that down too.

I put the notebook away in a drawer, under my things. I didn't want my mother to find it and start asking questions.

CHAPTER 11
AQUARIUM

It was almost summer and the days were getting longer and a lot warmer. The water in Mermary's basin was going down faster and I had to add water practically every day. Mermary loved to play in the water as it poured in from the hose, leaping out of the water and into the stream. I realized the basin was in the direct sunlight for several hours every day. On a really hot day, I put my finger in the water. It was very warm. Mermary was swimming slowly.

"Mermary, how is the water for you?"

"I like it for a while, but some days it gets too hot, and I can't cool down."

I noticed something else as well. She was growing. In fact, she didn't go inside the helmet shell anymore, and it was probably because she didn't fit.

I got an idea. I went inside and down to the basement, looking for an old aquarium we used to keep a sick lizard in. It was still there, dusty, but large, and more important, much deeper than the drain's basin. I found my mother in the kitchen cutting veggies for our dinner.

"Mom, can I get a goldfish or something? I can put it in that aquarium we have in the basement."

She put down the knife and looked at me.

"Yes, I think you're old enough to be responsible for a fish now. I've noticed that you've been spending a lot of time looking into the open drain outside. An aquarium will help you to see the fish better."

I hadn't realized she'd noticed me hanging out by the open drain. We went into the basement to bring up the aquarium and she washed it for me. I was so excited about making a comfortable home for Mermary and getting a fish too, which would be as much for Mermary as for me. I went out to talk to her.

"What do you think about coming inside to live with me? We could regulate the temperature of the water and you would be more comfortable."

"What's an 'aquarium'?" Mermary asked.

"It's a place full of water where fish and plants live. The water will be much cleaner, and you'll be able to see where I live."

"I would like to see the aquarium where you live," Mermary said.

I laughed. "I don't live in an aquarium." So then I explained about humans living differently from mer-people.

"Can we go now?"

"No, the aquarium isn't ready yet. I have to get some supplies and stuff before I introduce you to a new environment."

"What's an environment?" Mermary asked.

"It's a place where an animal or person lives. Different animals need a particular kind of place to live, like you need water, and I need air and a dry place."

I had to answer a lot more questions Mermary had. I didn't mind, I just hoped Mermary would like her new home and would want to stay there.

CHAPTER 12
A NEW HOME FOR MERMARY

That week my mom brought home a pump, a filter, sand, and other aquarium supplies.

"The water needs to be prepared ahead of time so it can be conditioned before the fish are introduced," she said. "If we set it up today, we can get your fish this weekend. Have you thought about where the aquarium should be?"

I had, of course. "My room."

So she carried the aquarium upstairs for me and put it on my desk, which was in a bay window. A bay is a part of a house with windows that projects out so the room gets extra light.

My mom explained each item and why fish needed it.

"The air pump circulates water so it doesn't get stagnant. The filter helps to clean the water of old food and waste produced by the fish, but you'll also have to clean the water frequently."

Next she showed me how to clean the sand with an aquarium vacuum and aerate it with my hand to take out any air pockets.

"Bacteria that are harmful to the fish can grow in air pockets," she told me.

I went to bed that night with the pump running. I was so excited I could barely sleep. Mermary was coming inside to live with me!

Finally the weekend came and we went to a pet store. I looked at the fish in all the different tanks and finally decided to start with two guppies. I chose the most beautiful ones the store had: one was blue and orange with spots and had a large, wavy tail and top fin. The other was blue and green with a yellow zebra tail. Of course, they cost twice as much the other, plainer guppies. I also got a lot of plants and two different kinds of food.

"That's a lot of greenery, honey," my mom said. "You're going to have an underwater jungle. Plus they'll grow. And why buy so much food? Why don't you get more fish instead?"

I shook my head. "I want the guppies to feel like they're in a real pond."

Of course, I had another very important reason for wanting all the plants. I knew my mother would be checking on how I was taking care of the fish. All the greenery was so Mermary would have a place to hide.

At home I had to float the plastic bag with guppies in the tank until the temperature in the bag and the aquarium were the same. My mother told me that's called entropy. It's so the fish don't get shocked and die. While I did that, I arranged the plants in the sand at the bottom of the tank. I also put an abalone shell in the bottom of the tank for Mermary's bed. After about half an hour my mother said I could set the guppies free.

I watched, but they took their time swimming out of the bag. Finally one swam out and the other followed after a minute. I was impatient to bring Mermary in, but I still had to wait. I couldn't let my mom see me bringing a mermaid into the house. I knew she was going to run some errands, but she was taking her time about leaving, cleaning the drawers in the kitchen, straightening the items in them, throwing things out. I helped because it gave me something to do while I waited for her to go.

Finally all the drawers were tidy. She went to change her blouse and get her purse and keys. I went to the front room and when she came in, I was sitting with a book open on my lap.

"Would you like to go to Kmart with me?" she asked.

"No, I have to read this book for school."

"Okay. Is there anything you want while I'm out?"

I shook my head.

"What would you like for dinner?"

I thought I was going to start crying if she didn't go. I couldn't think about food right then. I forced myself to be patient and said, "How about popcorn?"

"You silly," my mother said. "How about if I make hamburgers?"

Hamburgers was one of my favorite meals, so I acted happy, otherwise she was going to know something was strange and never leave. After I watched her car go down the street and turn the corner, I got the plastic bag and ran outside.

"The aquarium is ready," I told Mermary. "You can come inside now!"

Mermary did a somersault in the water and then did something I hadn't seen before. She leapt high out of the water and did a dive from midair.

"That was beautiful Mermary!" I said.

"Thank you!"

I put the plastic bag in the water and after it filled, Mermary swam right in. I put a knot at the end and headed into the house. Mermary swam around the bag, touching the plastic and putting her face up close to the side to look at everything.

I opened the top of the aquarium and floated the bag at the top of the water, but Mermary swam around impatiently, pushing her face into the side of bag and punching it.

"Let me out of here," she demanded.

"I think we need to wait until the water in the bag is the same as the water in the tank," I told her.

"Let me out," Mermary yelled and hammered at the plastic.

So I opened the bag and she swam out at once. The different temperatures didn't seem to bother her at all.

"I couldn't breathe in that bag," she told me. "I didn't like it."

Then she dove and swam straight to the bottom, then from one end of the aquarium to the other with her arms out in front of her, weaving in and out of the plants, touching them, and once, taking a nip. She swam up to each guppy and stared at them. The fish, who were afraid of me, had no fear of the mermaid. Mermary reached out one webbed hand and stroked one of the fish, then she chased it, making me laugh.

I got the fish food and sprinkled a little in. The guppies ate, but after snacking on a few, Mermary went back to investigating her new home. She sampled a couple more plants as she swam through them, leaving tiny nicks in the sides. Before I put the lid back on the tank, Mermary did another leap in the air.

"I love my new home," she said. "The water is so fresh and clear, plus I have room to dive! And there's a beautiful forest and fish!"

"I'm glad you like it," I said. "But I have to warn you about something."

"What is it?"

"No one else can know about you. I put all those plants in there so you would have a place to hide if someone other than me comes in here. Will you do that?"

"That's what I did when I first saw you," Mermary said. "Remember? I did it automatically." "Automatically" was a word I had taught her.

"In this case, you did it instinctively. That means something deep down inside told you I might be dangerous, so you hid. That's what you should do if anybody other than me comes near the tank," I said.

She promised she would.

Now Mermary would be close to me whenever I was in my room. Best of all, I could talk to her whenever I wanted.

CHAPTER 13
LIVING WITH A MERMAID

I learned even more about Mermary when I spent the whole day with her. For example, she always knew when I was coming, because she could tell my footsteps from my mother and father's. Also, she could hear me perfectly well through the water and glass of her tank. I learned that sometimes she didn't want to interrupt her swimming to talk. She would swim from one end of the tank to the other and back again, sometimes making a detour to the bottom or top. Other times she'd get quiet and sit in the abalone shell at the bottom. I figured out it was a form of napping for her, although she did it with her eyes open. Actually, they weren't exactly open. She covered them with a clear membrane that went over her eyes. It's called a nictitating membrane, like in the corner of cats' eyes when they're sleepy. They protect her eyes in the water, and because they're clear, she could still see perfectly well.

She was also was very active at night and wanted the curtains open so she could look at the night sky and out at the ocean. My mother had told me to keep them closed during the day because the sun would cause algae to grow faster, but Mermary scrubbed the algae off the glass and ate it, so it wasn't a problem.

She told me that the moon affected water.

"The water changes at different times of the month."

"How?"

"Well, sometimes it's heavy, or thick, and harder to swim through. Other times it's thin, and I can swim faster. Sometimes there's a sort of cloudiness, like the water has something in it."

All this was information I added to my mermaid diary.

I was always thinking about Mermary and what she might like. For example, at the hardware store I found an end piece of new pine board about five inches by seven. I wondered if Mermary could use it as a raft, and brought it home. Mermary sniffed it all over. The only time I ever saw her sniff anything was when I brought food for her. Then she got up on it and after that, dove from it all the time. Sometimes she'd stretch out her top half under the light with her tail trailing in the water, lifting it out occasionally and using it to sprinkle or splash herself with water.

One day I was with my mom running an errand on the street nearest the beach. She gave me permission to go down by the beach as long as I stayed away from the waves. I looked in the sand until I found rocks worn smooth by the ocean. One had different layers in it and holes. I also found some clam shells and even a couple of little cone shells. Mermary loved the new additions. She swam around and around them and through the holes in the rock, then surfaced.

"Did those shells and rocks come from the ocean?"

"Well, they came from the beach, but before that they were in the ocean. How did you know?"

"They smell like it, only stronger."

Of course, even I could smell the ocean from where we lived, a block from the ocean. The aquarium was looking more like a mermaid's home.

Mermary asked a lot of questions about the sea, like how big it was, how deep, what lived there. I tried to find answers for the questions I didn't know. When I found pictures in National Geographic, I would open the magazine and prop it up against the side of the aquarium so Mermary could look at them. Once I found a wonderful picture of underground water with someone swimming in it. Mermary stared at it for a long time.

"Can you take me to the ocean?" she asked.

I told her I would someday, when she was bigger. I wanted to be sure she'd be able to survive by herself in the ocean. I had seen documentaries of baby turtles breaking out of their eggs and climbing up, out of the sand, then being eaten immediately by birds and other predators. I hated thinking about little mermaids being eaten the same way.

One day I brought out all my dolls. I told Mermary they were called toys, and human children played with them. I showed her my vintage Madam Alexander doll with long orange hair, a green dress, and straw hat.

"This one used to be my mother's. Her name is Holly." I picked up another one with thick, long black hair. "This one is a Latina Bratz doll. Her name is Isabel. And this one," I showed her my Barbie doll, "is Barbie-Ann."

I had a couple of tiny plastic dolls, and I put them on Mermary's raft. She took them into the water one at a time and swam around with them, showing them the different things she had in the tank. One of them sank to the bottom when she let go of it, but the other floated on its back or stomach. She finally finished playing with them, and put them back on the raft and lay down next to them. It was amazing to watch a mermaid play with dolls.

After that we made up games and played dolls together a lot. Before I started playing dolls with Mermary I didn't play with my dolls much anymore. But it was so much fun to play dolls with a mermaid, that we played practically every day!

CHAPTER 14
THE MOON AND DREAMS

After Mermary came inside, I started having lots of dreams. They were so clear, sometimes they seemed real. I often dreamed about swimming in the ocean, and sometimes I was a mermaid too, swimming with Mermary. I dreamed of other mermaids too. They were always Mermary's friends. They were all different, sometimes beautiful colors, sometimes dark colors, like mud. There were male mermaids too.

There would be strange fish in my dreams sometimes, like once I dreamed of a sea serpent-fish, and he guarded the mermaids in my dream. Another time I dreamed of a school of beautiful fish that looked like they were made out of glass, with turquoise eyes. Another time I dreamed of a funny fish that had legs and arms like a human and talked out of his fish mouth. Having Mermary near me was making me dream more.

I started getting up really early so we would have time to talk and tell each other what we dreamed. Sometimes she dreamed of me or the guppies, but more often she was swimming with lots of fish, in water that had no end to it, which of course was the ocean. She'd dream of other mermaids too, and having adventures with them. What was best of all was when we both had the same dream, or really similar. We called our dreams about the ocean "sea-dreaming."

One night Mermary and I were sitting in the dark, looking out at the full moon over the ocean. Mermary was sitting on her little raft, leaning against the side. She was in a quiet, dreamy mood. I was too, although in my case I was getting sleepy.

"I think dreams must come from the moon," Mermary said. "Because my dreams are different when the moon is full."

"Really? How?"

"They become more magical. Like I have wings and I'm flying over the ocean, or I'm growing legs and walking on land. Or I dream of you being able to breathe underwater, or turning into a mermaid. I feel different too, excited, like I can do anything. Remember that dream I had, where I was holding up a sword that glowed, and I was leading an invisible army of sea creatures? I felt brave and strong in that dream."

I wrote our dreams down in my mermaid journal. I also wrote down our ideas about them, and that *all* my dreams of Mermary seemed magical.

She loved the moon and sometimes sang to it. I loved hearing her tiny voice with no words. It was small enough that I didn't worry my parents would hear, and anyway if they did, I could say it was the radio.

I read that mermaids were connected to the moon. It made sense, since the moon controls the ocean tides. People knew so much about mermaids that I was sure, once upon a time, mermaids must have lived everywhere. Now the only information about them was in stories and art.

Another night Mermary said, "The moon is so beautiful. Sometimes I think the goddess of mermaids is a giant mermaid who lives at the bottom of the ocean. But other times, I think the mermaid goddess lives in the seas on the moon."

"The seas on the moon are dry," I told her.

"The moon seas must have once had water, but they dried up. Why else would they call them seas?" I didn't know how to answer that. "I think there's probably ghost water that mermaid spirits swim in. I think mermaids go to the moon to be with the Mermaid Goddess of the Moon after we die."

I thought that sounded beautiful, but I didn't want to think about mermaids dying, especially Mermary. "What made you think about all those things?" I asked.

"I think about lots of things when I watch the moon at night, after you go to sleep. You've read me mermaid stories, and told me that mythology is the story of gods and where we came from. So that's what I think about."

The Catholic religion taught that there was one God who made everything. I hadn't thought about mermaids having their own god or goddess, but it made sense since most of the people on earth had their own religion, and their own kind of God.

I wrote in my log, "mermaids have wonderful imaginations," and "mermaids are spiritual."

CHAPTER 15
SCHOOL LETS OUT

School got out for the summer. The past two summers I had a babysitter during the day. That year I was old enough to stay by myself, I just had to call and get permission before I went anywhere. I was glad. The one last year was nosy, and would have found out about Mermary for sure. The one the year before that just surfed the Internet most of the time and I was bored.

Part of the reason why I didn't have to have a sitter was because I was enrolled in summer school. It didn't start for a couple of weeks after regular school finished. I got lots of books from the library and convinced my mother to let me stay home and read them. I also promised I wouldn't watch TV unless I got her permission. But I had something much more fun to do than spend my time watching television.

I read to Mermary and told her stories, and put on the radio so we could dance—I didn't really know how to dance so they were actually exercises I'd seen on TV and Mermary would copy most of what I did. I brought my lunch up on a tray to share with her and the guppies, and we played dolls a lot. Every day I put Mermary in a glass pitcher that's sort of like the one on Kool-Aid packages and carried her around the house so she could get a better look at where I lived. She also watched a special program with me on the National Geographic channel that my mother said I could see every day.

My mom asked me if I was bored during the day while she was away.

"No way!" I said.

CHAPTER 16
SUMMER SCHOOL

On my first day of summer school, I said goodbye to Mermary before I left and put my lips up to the side of the tank to kiss her through the glass. She came to the glass on the other side and kissed me back.

"I'll be back after one o'clock," I told her. She could see my digital clock from the tank, and of course I had taught her to read the time. "My mom won't be home for a couple of hours, so we'll have lots of time to hang out then."

"Are you excited about school?" she asked.

"Sort of," I said. "But it's not my regular school, and I won't know anyone."

"You'll probably get to know some of the kids," she said.

"Yeah, probably," I said, although I doubted it.

My mother drove me to a large community center on the other side of town on her way to work.

"Have a good time," she said. "Try to make some friends, Cammie. You could invite them over." She always said that. Today she added, "People need friends. They're part of your personal resources."

"What does that mean?"

"Well, sometimes you need a friend to tell things to. Sometimes they help you figure things out, or do favors for you. And you do the same for them. Friends make you feel better about yourself, and not so alone."

I said I would try, and she kissed me and I got out of the car. I looked around. It was sunny but not hot yet. The community center was large, with a glass front, and there were kids everywhere. I didn't know how to make friends, and I wished I wasn't so quiet all the time.

My first class was Dance and Movement. I was worried it was going to be hard, but it was easy and fun. We started by stretching, "to get all the yawns out."

"Come on, everyone!" Miss Calista, the teacher, said. "Stretch, and don't be afraid to yawn!" She stretched her arms and legs and bent backward and forward and opened her mouth and made loud noises when she yawned. We all copied her, and some kids laughed, but she didn't mind. Then she taught us some yoga positions.

The next class was creative writing, where Mr. Mildigger taught us to write a poem, which was easy because we could choose whatever topic we wanted, and then use a kind of formula to write the poem. We were supposed to start the poem with "if I were," and it didn't have to rhyme. I wrote,

> If I were a mermaid
> I would live in the ocean
> With my mermaid friend
> And we would swim together
> For a thousand years.

I didn't know that after we wrote the poems, we were going to have to read them out loud. The teacher called on me.

I was afraid Mr. Mildigger would say I didn't really have a mermaid friend, but instead he said, "Very nice use of imagination. Boys and girls, you can always write about made up things, like Camile did."

We wrote another poem, then it was time to go to the next class, which was art. We had to draw apples and bananas with charcoal. Miss Cavanaugh, the teacher, showed us how to draw their shapes, and then put shading in so our drawings looked "realistic." She used a lamp with a bright light and a shade to shine on an apple so we could see the shadows it made. The charcoal was messy and we had to wash our hands before we went to lunch.

After art we went into a big room for lunch that was being set up for us on turquoise-and-coral colored trays. We each got a sandwich, cookie, orange, and container of milk. I sat at a long table between two girls, but they were both talking to the person next to them on their other side. I looked at the girl across from me and said, "hello," but I don't think she could hear me because it was so noisy.

Our last class was science. It was about green ecology. A really nice guy with long hair tied back into a pony tail introduced himself as Green Jerry. He wore an orange T-shirt with "THINK GREEN" on it. He gave each one of us a pair of bright orange gloves that we were supposed to write our names on with big black marking pens.

"How many of you do recycling?" he asked. Only a few kids raised their hands. We did recycling at home, but I didn't raise my hand because I was afraid he'd call on me. "Well, today you're going to learn all about it. Follow me."

He took us out in back of the community center and brought over the receptacles and the garbage barrel we had used after lunch and dumped it all out on a tarp.

"Garbage and trash is not the same thing, kids, even though people sometimes use the words interchangeably," he told us. "Garbage is old food, fruit and vegetable peelings, bones, stuff like that. Trash is junk you can't use anymore that gets thrown away, broken toys, plastic things that can't be recycled, or what you might have after you eat fast food. But a lot of things that get put into the trash can be put into the green barrel, which is for composting. Learn good green habits. Green living starts when you sort what's left over after you eat."

He had us put on the gloves and start sorting everything on the tarp and putting them in the correct barrels. Before I knew it, class was over. We stowed the gloves where he told us, and kids started going home. I went out front where there were shuttles that I was supposed to take home.

As soon as I got there, I ran up to my room. Mermary got up on her raft and I told her about my first day. I showed her the yoga positions we had learned, and it was pretty easy to remember because they were connected.

"We get on our hands and knees like this—this is called Table position." Then I arched my back. "This is cat pose," then I bent my back in the other direction, "and this is cow."

Mermary climbed further up out of the water and, bending her tail about where her knees would be, she copied what I did as well as she could.

"The teacher said the stretching and yoga was to warm up, and then she told us to follow her in a line around the classroom and do whatever she did."

I couldn't remember exactly what the teacher had done so I made some stuff up. This time Mermary jumped into the water and copied me. I stopped to put on some music, and we both danced around. I kept laughing because sometimes Mermary looked funny dancing. But sometimes she looked really beautiful and I would stop to watch her. It was totally awesome.

Then I showed her my drawings and explained about shading. She didn't get it very well, probably because my drawings weren't very good. So I went and found a flashlight and got a tennis ball and shone the light on the ball the way the teacher had, and then Mermary understood.

I got out my poems and I read them to her. She loved the mermaid poem. I read the second one I did:

> Moon, moon
> You're coming soon
> Right now you're just a smile
> In the sky.

"I didn't know how to write the second half of my poem, but the teacher said we could always go back and change it."

Mermary thought for a minute, then said, "How about . . . ?"

> Moon, Full Moon
> Coming soon.
> You're just a smile
> In early June.

"Mermary! How did you think of that so fast?"

"It just came to me."

I got a pencil and wrote down the improved poem on the same page as the first poem. Mermary was going into one her resting moods, and I was tired too. I crossed my arms and laid my head down on the desk to rest for a minute.

"Camile?" It was my mother.

I opened my eyes and sat up quickly to look at the tank, but all I could see was the forest of greenery and the two guppies swimming in and out of them. Mermary was nowhere in sight.

"I'm sorry, honey, I didn't mean to scare you. Why are you sleeping at your desk?"

"I just put my head down to rest. I guess I fell asleep."

"What have you got on your face?"

I got up to look in the mirror. "It's charcoal. From art."

"How was your first day at summer school?" She was looking at the papers on my desk, but I was scared for her to be so close to Mermary, so I picked them up and gave them to her.

"School was fun." I went to the bathroom to wash my face. My mother followed me, just like I hoped she would.

"Tell me about these, Cammie." She was going through the pages.

"Okay. Can I get some lemonade?"

"Of course."

We went downstairs to the kitchen. My mother was amazed about the poems, especially the one Mermary helped me with. I had to let her think I wrote it.

"You should take this to school and show the teacher how you re-wrote the poem," my mom said.

I shrugged and said, "Okay," but I knew I wouldn't. I was afraid he'd make me read it out loud, and I hated that.

CHAPTER 17
SHOPPING

One of the things my mother and I did together was go to garage sales and thrift stores. Sometimes she needed to get clothes for work because the ones she had were ruined or worn out, and she didn't want to wear new clothes and get them dirty. I looked at books and toys, but first I would always look to see if there was anything I could get for Mermary. I found a little ceramic castle that I knew was made for an aquarium because it was with other aquarium things like a bag of sand with a bunch of shells and a piece of white coral, which I also got.

I also found a little doll hand mirror. The mirror part was round and the handle and frame was silver plastic with curlicues in it, which sort of looked like waves. I knew from reading about mermaids that they sometimes had mirrors, and in one story I read, a mermaid used her mirror to predict the future. I had also noticed that Mermary sometimes looked at herself in the top of the water when she swam slowly up to it.

I gave it to Mermary, and she sat on the raft and had to hold it in both her hands. She tried to touch the face in the mirror. It was funny.

"Cammie, what is this?"

"Mermary, that's a mirror, and you're looking at yourself. It's like what I have—" I pointed at the mirror on the wall. "I was able to find one in your size."

"I thought it was a little TV at first."

Mermary played with the mirror, looking at herself all over. As I watched her, I noticed that Mermary was growing. She was much bigger than when I first found her. Not just longer (she was more than five inches now), but bigger all around. She was almost as thick as my little finger. The fin at the end of her tail was developing too into a fan shape.

After a while Mermary dove with the mirror into the water and held it in front of herself as she swam through the tank, watching to see how she looked when she swam. She went up to each fish and tried to hold the mirror in front of them, but after nibbling at the edges, they lost interest. They didn't care what they looked like.

Mermary swam down to the bottom of the tank and stuck the handle into the sand and lay in front of it, studying her reflection, turning her head this way and that and sometimes shaking her head to see what her hair looked like, or moving her tail and curling it over her. It was really interesting to watch her studying herself. I used to think my mother's biological work must be boring, but now I could understand why she loved it so much.

I had been excited when I found the mirror, but the best thing of all was when I found a mermaid doll at a Salvation Army. She was about six inches long and had big painted eyes and long, light green hair. At her waist was a tiny comb attached to a string around her waist, and her bottom half was a tail with shimmery, metallic blue-green fabric with pink that showed when you turned her a certain way. Mermary would love it!

When my mother was done shopping she looked to see what I had found.

"I thought you stopped playing with dolls, Camile," she said.

"It's so pretty," was all I could think of to say. Of course I couldn't tell her why I really wanted it.

When I got home I ran upstairs to show it to Mermary.

"Mermary, look what I found for you!"

I was able to bend the doll's tail so she could sit on the raft partly in the water, like Mermary. Mermary jumped onto the raft fast and splashy like she usually did, and the doll tipped over and fell in the water. Mermary dove in after her and rescued her. Even though the doll was a bigger than Mermary, she didn't seem to have a problem bringing her back to the surface, although I had to help put her back on the raft.

"Let's think of a name for her," I said. I mentioned a lot of names. "How about Sita."

"How about Sea-li?" Mermary said.

"That's perfect, Mermary!"

So that became her name. Mermary talked to Sea-li the way she talked to me, or the way we talked to my dolls. After a while Mermary went down into the little fish castle and brought up the tiny doll I had given her that didn't float.

"Let's play dolls!" she said. "Sea-li will be my mermaid friend, and this will be her baby."

I got out my dolls. Only one of them had a bathing suit. I walked one doll up to the other.

"Why don't we go to the beach to look for mermaids, Holly?" I said in doll talk.

"Okay. Let me put on my bathing suit." I changed Holly into her bathing suit and got a sun hat for Isabel, then I walked them toward the tank. Mermary was sitting on the raft with Sea-li and the tiny doll.

Holly: "Oh, look! There are some mermaids now!"

Isabel: "Let's go talk to them!" I moved them up to the top of the tank. "Hello, what are your names?"

"I'm Mermary, and this is my friend, Sea-li," Mermary said.

"Are those baby mermaids?"

"Yes," Mermary said. "They haven't grown their tails yet."

We were having so much fun I didn't hear my mother coming. Mermary suddenly disappeared into the seaweed. Then I heard a tap on the door and my mother came in.

"Mom!"

"Hi, Cammie, what are you doing?" I looked at the tank, but Mermary blended in perfectly with the seaweed forest. Sea-li was rocking gently on the raft, next to the two baby mermaids. "You're playing with your dolls."

I nodded.

She came over and looked at them. It seemed like she was a little upset, but I didn't know why. She looked into the aquarium at Mermary's raft and the dolls still sitting on it.

After a moment, she sighed. "You haven't watered the garden or done your other chores."

"I'm sorry," I said. "I'll do them right now."

But I could tell that wasn't what was bothering her. She was still looking at my dolls. I checked again, but Mermary was nowhere in sight.

That evening I went to the kitchen to get my bedtime snack and I heard my mother in the living room, talking on her phone.

"She's playing with dolls again! And not only that, but she talks to her fish . . ." Of course, I couldn't hear what the other person said. "It's just that I think she's too old for imaginary playmates . . . well, yes, I guess it is good that she's talking more . . . I'm just afraid she's regressing." That was a word I would have to look up.

" . . . I'm not sure what the age range is. I stopped playing with dolls when I was about seven . . . I know, I just worry she isn't developing the way she should . . . Why can she talk to her dolls, and not to other children? . . . Do you think I should take them away from her?"

Take them away?

I tip-toed back to my room so she wouldn't catch me listening. I got my dictionary and looked up "regressing." It meant to go back to an earlier stage of development. I wondered how playing with dolls again meant I was regressing. Lots of girls in my class played with dolls. They talked about collecting Bratz dolls and getting clothes for them, or the different kinds of American Dolls and outfits they could get. One girl was always bragging that she had more than fifty dolls.

Actually, it wasn't exactly true that I had stopped playing with them. Before Mermary, I didn't play with dolls as much as I used to when I was little. And sometimes I slept with a doll or one of my stuffed animals, which are doll animals. But now that I had Mermary, it was so much more fun to play with them. I didn't know how to let my mother know it was all right. I worried about her taking them away from us. I decided to put the dolls away after I played with them, instead of leaving them out to keep Mermary company when I wasn't there.

CHAPTER 18
THE MERMAID WEBSITE

"Camile, I have to run some errands. Want to go with me?"

It was Saturday, and I had other ideas. "Can I go to the library?"

"Sure."

I liked it when my mother left me at the library while she did something else. I used the computers to look up mermaids. I couldn't do it at home too much because my mother checked the history. Even though she had never said anything, I knew she didn't like my interest in mermaids. She only liked subjects that were true and scientific.

I searched the library catalog and got 243 items about mermaids! I was confused why my list was so different from Ms. Tanglewood's, but when I actually looked at the books, it seemed like most of them weren't really about mermaids. Some just had "mermaid" in the title, like one about a man with a yacht called *The White Mermaid*. One with the title *Mermaid Island*, wasn't a place where mermaids lived, and didn't even have mermaids in it; it was some kind of spy story about a missile testing site. Those were adult books, and I finally figured out there were two catalogs, one for adults and one for children. The adult catalog included all the children's titles. That's why so many more titles came up than I had on Ms. Tanglewood's list.

The library had just opened when my mother dropped me off, so it wasn't busy yet. I sneaked and got on my favorite adult computer, which was behind a pillar so the librarians couldn't see me from their desk. One of them, Ms. Brady (who I secretly thought of as Miss Bratty), was always kicking me off and sending me to the children's computers. But the children's computer had a filter and prevented me from going to a lot of sites.

The first thing I did was check a web page called "Do You Believe in Mermaids," where I had been reading postings. My mother didn't want me posting messages without her checking the website first, but this was just a site where people were debating whether mermaids were real or not. There were two columns. On one side the people who believed in mermaids posted, and the other side were the ones who didn't. The believers talked about sighting mermaids, or gave reasons why they believed in them. The non-believers wrote all the reasons why mermaids were impossible or ridiculous. Sometimes the posters argued with each other.

I had posted for the first time a few weeks back. I said mermaids were real, because I found one. It was exciting, partly because I was able to tell people about Mermary, and partly because they believed in mermaids. Since everyone used a made up name on the site, I used Sea Bee to disguise my real initials. I had written:

> "Mermaids are real. I found one in a puddle after a storm near the beach. I think she came out of an egg."—Sea Bee

Questions had popped up right away, and I had answered:

> "A puddle? How big is she?"—Island Girl
> "3 inches when I found her."—Sea Bee
> "She has grown. She is 5 inches now."—Sea Bee

> "Did u c egg?"—Undine
> "Saw an egg shell."—Sea Bee

> "Y in puddle?"—Island Girl
> "Luna Beach flooded during storms."—Sea Bee
> "Where is she now?"—Sirena T
> "My house in a tank."—Sea Bee

Since then, there were lots of new posts, people asking more questions and telling me to post pictures of her. On the disbelieving side, people said things like:

> "Right, a 3 in. mermaid."—Waterman
> "I don't believe you. Prove it."—Navy Jones
> "Anyone can say anything on the internet."—Aqua Lung
> "No response. C.B. lying."—Navy Jones

I realized my handle didn't fool anyone.

A guy on the believing side posted,

> "I blv u. but wrong to keep mermaid. Luna Be. 1 hr from Monterey Co. Donate mermade 2 Monterey Bay Acquarium so we cn c her."—Sea Cowboy

A lot of people on both sides agreed with Sea Cowboy.

> "Sea Cowboy is right. How are you going to take care of her so she will survive? The aquarium people will provide the right environment for her."—Sirena T

Then someone who called himself Pirate Andy Kydd wrote

> "I KNOW WHERE LUNA BEACH IS, AND IT'S NOT BIG. BET I CAN TRACK YOU DOWN, THEN WE'LL HAVE A LOOK AT THIS MERMAID OF YOURS."

That got me really scared. Everyone said the Internet was anonymous, but I knew that some e-mails and stuff on the Internet could be traced. Could Pirate Andy Kydd really find me? Now I knew why my mother didn't think the Internet was safe and guarded the computer at home. There were a lot more questions and some posters begged me to say more, but I decided not to post there again. I left the site.

After that I found an article titled, "The Mermaid Mystery." It was about a team of scientists who went to an island in Indonesia because the native people said they had mermaids in their bay. They called them ilkai. The scientists watched and searched the waters, and finally discovered what the Indonesian people were actually seeing were dugongs, which are sea mammals related to manatees. I knew about manatees because I read that a lot of sailors have mistaken them for mermaids. Dugongs don't look anything like mermaids. In fact, they're related to elephants.

I looked up—*uh oh*, Miss Bratty was making a beeline for me, and she looked cross. I looked around and saw all the adult computers were full now.

"You know you're not supposed to be using the adults' computers, Camile," she scolded. "What are you looking at?"

"A story about dugongs," I said. She could see I was telling the truth, because there was a diagram of dugong sizes compared to a man. "I can't get this on the children's computer."

I wasn't sure if this was true, but she calmed down. Last time she caught me, I was looking at mermaid cartoons.

"How about if I print it out so you can read it, and we can let an adult use this computer," she said. She printed it out and gave it to me, and didn't charge me, which was really nice because she's usually so crabby.

I went to pick up the books I ordered. One was actually a magazine, and the other was a book on how to draw mermaids.

My mother still wasn't back, so I wandered into the reference section, where I saw different kinds of dictionaries and encyclopedias. I looked up mermaid in a nautical encyclopedia. It said that although mermaids were mythical, sailors had been sighting them all over the world for centuries, which sounded contradictory to me.

An Encyclopedia of Piracy said pirates and mermaids had a long history, and there were some pirates who actually had mermaid girlfriends. Good mermaids saved men from drowning, granted wishes, and sometimes led them to treasure. The bad ones put curses on people, made storms, and sank ships. Some kinds of mermaids lured men to them with their beauty and singing, then drowned and ate them. It said that while there were some good mermaids, mostly they were bad and it warned pirates to stay away from them.

A dictionary on folklore said mermaids were connected to fairies and seals, were believed to be magic, and that many cultures had tales and songs about mermaids. It also said there were stories about mermaids turning into humans and coming on land, and that some of them married and had families.

A dictionary of symbols said mermaids could be symbolic of bad luck or intuition, which is when you know something deep down inside, without anyone telling you. Mirrors, combs, and harps were connected with mermaids, which had been in some of the tales I'd read. Mermaids were connected with the moon and could sometimes tell the future.

"There you are!" I looked up. It was my mother. "I've been looking all over for you!"

I was in an aisle, sitting on the floor with the books, so I got up and started putting them away.

"What are you looking up, Cammie?" she asked. She picked up the encyclopedia on archeology.

"There are so many encyclopedias," I hedged. "I can use them for homework."

My mother smiled at the nautical encyclopedia. I knew she wanted me to go into a research field like hers. Maybe I would. I could be a woman sailor-scientist and do research on mermaids.

CHAPTER 19
BULLY GIRL

I loved summer school and couldn't wait to get there every day. Miss Calista said I was very flexible and I was good at doing the positions. She chose me to demonstrate yoga positions a lot. I didn't mind because I didn't have to say anything. One day I noticed a girl at the back of the class looking angry. Her name was Libby and I had seen her picking on some of the kids. She was big and had frizzy brown hair that always needed to be combed, and she wore glasses with thick brown frames. Miss Calista sometimes got after her because she didn't stand straight. Libby would straighten up for as long as Miss Calista was watching, and as soon as she turned away, Libby would slouch again and make a face.

We lined up for lunch that day, and Libby cut in line in front of me. I didn't say anything but the boy behind me yelled at her.

"Hey, no cutting, Libby! Get at the back of the line!"

She pointed at me. "She was saving my place, so there." Then she gave me a warning look like she was going to get me if I said anything.

The boy behind me poked me in the back and grumbled, "It isn't fair to save places. What if everyone did that? You'd be at the back of the line, starving."

I didn't say anything of course. Sometimes I got in trouble because I didn't stick up for myself. When I told my parents about stuff that happened, my mother would say, "Use your words, Cammie. People are going to pick on you if you let them."

But my father had told me, "Sometimes it's better to keep quiet when things like that happen. Keep your own counsel. People will eventually find out the truth."

Luckily it didn't happen very often because I always behaved, plus people didn't notice me. I thought of it as protective coloring, like animals that are hard to see because they match the environment and keep really still.

But it seemed like that was changing, because the summer school teachers called on me a lot. At first it was really hard to get up in front of everyone. Like one day when Miss Calista gave everyone a Japanese character and made us get in front, one by one, and try to take the shape of the character. It was easier when I thought about going home and demonstrating the character to Mermary, so when it was my turn I did my best.

Lunch that day was an egg salad sandwich, a chocolate cookie, and bananas. Libby's banana had brown spots. Mine was bright yellow, with some green. After I got my tray, Libby came over and grabbed my banana, then put hers on my tray and ran away laughing. I didn't mind because I actually prefer bananas with spots. Sometimes the yellow ones taste green.

While we were all eating lunch, I saw Libby sitting with her friends. Libby noticed me looking at her and she started whispering in Nancy's ear, who was sitting next to her. Then they both looked at me and laughed. Libby was probably telling her about the banana, and I thought they were being silly because it wasn't a big deal, and it wasn't even funny.

After lunch was our class with Green Jerry, which he always made really fun. That week he was teaching us about compost. I had noticed Libby wouldn't do any of the jobs Green Jerry gave us, even though they were all really simple. She just sat in the shade while everyone else worked. But on this day he saw her.

"Hey Libby," he called. "Grab the hose and put some water on this garbage, will you?"

Libby made a face and took her time getting the hose.

I was helping to tear up newspaper with some other kids, and Nancy was talking to Gigi, who was one of the other girls who hung out with Libby.

"Look at Libby," Nancy said to Gigi. "She's so lazy, and now that Green Jerry is making her to do something, she's moving really slow."

"I know. She always does that," Gigi said back.

I was surprised, because I thought they were Libby's best friends. She was always sitting with them.

Then Gigi said, "I can't stand her. Just because we go to the same school, she acts like we're best friends. I don't know how to get rid of her."

"I know," Nancy said. "She always invites herself when we do something."

"Oh, I never tell her," Gigi said.

"Yeah, but a lot of times she figures it out, like that time we went to the children's matinee, and she invited herself along."

Gigi looked over at me, but I pretended like I wasn't paying attention. I gathered up a bunch of paper and took it over to the pile of garbage that Green Jerry was preparing for compost. Libby was scattering water from the hose over it, then all of a sudden squirted me. I didn't get very wet because the water wasn't on very high, but Green Jerry saw.

"Libby, cut that out. That's not very nice," he said.

"She looked hot," Libby said, although she looked glad that she'd done it.

I actually opened my mouth and said, "I don't mind. It *is* hot."

Then Libby looked mad, but I didn't know why since I kept her from getting in trouble. After a minute she threw down the hose. "I'm going to tear paper with my friends."

Green Jerry asked me to water in her place, and while I was doing it, I saw Libby sitting between Nancy and Gigi and letting them do all the work. I think she was talking about some of the kids because she would point and say something, and they would all laugh. Actually, Libby laughed and Nancy kind of smiled, but Gigi didn't even smile.

After school when the shuttle was full and taking off, I saw Libby walking home. She walked funny, slouching as usual, and she looked hot and sad. There was a gang of six or seven kids in front of her talking and laughing. She tried to catch up with them, but one of them saw her and said something, and they all ran away.

When I got home I told Mermary about my day like I always did, and a big part of it was about Libby.

"I used to think Libby was popular, because she hangs around some popular girls, but it turns out they don't like her," I told Mermary. I thought about the gang of kids running away from her. "I guess she's just horning in on people. I've heard people call her Lub the Tub, or Tubby Lubby, making fun of her."

"Maybe Libby is mean because kids are mean to her," Mermary said.

That actually made sense. Mermary was really smart sometimes.

"I can tell Libby hates it when teachers call on her, because she doesn't pay attention and usually doesn't know what we're talking about. And she hates to get up in front of the movement class."

"Why?" Mermary asked.

"I'm not sure, maybe she feels self-conscious, like I do. Once the teacher set the room up with furniture and demonstrated how she wanted us to dance around them, using them as props. Then she chose Libby and two other girls to perform for us. The girls did okay, but I think Libby was trying to be funny because she made faces and danced like a monkey, and the teacher said she was just being silly."

"What did Libby say?"

"Nothing. She just shrugged her shoulders and sat down. The next day, she didn't go to class. After Movement I went to the bathroom, and Libby was in there sitting on the sink, chewing gum. She said, 'I hate dance class.' Then she asked if she was in trouble because she didn't go to class. I said I didn't know, and she said, 'Is Miss Calista looking for me?' And I said I didn't think the teacher even noticed. So Libby says, 'I better not go out yet because she might be out there.'"

"She was hoping the teacher missed her, and maybe felt sorry for her," Mermary said.

"Really?" I had noticed Mermary had intuition, because she was always telling me things she figured out about people.

"Yes. Why else would she be asking those questions about your teacher?"

"Maybe Miss Calista was actually glad Libby wasn't there. Libby gets on everyone's nerves, and it seems like no one likes her." I knew what it was like to have no friends, even if it was for completely different reasons. But I, at least, had Mermary.

"You know what, Mermary? I feel sorry for her. I think she does all that stuff trying to make friends, but it just makes people not like her more."

"Why don't *you* be friends with her?" Mermary asked.

"Me? But . . . I don't know how to make friends."

"Yes, you do," she said. "You just start talking to them, like you did with me."

CHAPTER 20
LEARNING TO MAKE FRIENDS

The next week I went to school and decided I was going to be nice to Libby. So I went and sat next to her in writing class. She glared at me, but after that didn't pay any attention to me. I sat next to her again in art, but she didn't seem to notice.

In the lunch room after I got my tray, I saw Libby sitting by herself. I went over but she put her hands on the seats next to her and said, "Saved," so I sat at another table. Gigi and Nancy came through the line, but when Libby waved at them, they pretended not to see her and sat with some other girls.

The next morning I waited to see where Libby sat, then went and sat next to her. I said "hi," but she either didn't hear me or was ignoring me. People not noticing you was almost the same as being ignored, so I didn't know which it was.

"Okay, class, today I'm going to have you spell out the letters of the alphabet with your bodies," Miss Calista said. "For instance, I'm going to show you 'I.'" She stood straight and held one of her hands made into a fist over her head. "Think about the letters of the alphabet and how you might get into its shape. Some letters will probably need two people. Now, who would like to try first?"

Nobody raised their hand. She looked around the class. "Camile? Why don't you and Libby come up here and do 'A'?"

Libby turned and gave me a really annoyed look. Miss Calista often called on me to demonstrate, so Libby probably thought it was my fault she got called on since I was sitting next to her. I started going up to the front.

Libby stayed in her seat. "I don't know how."

"Camile, can you show her?"

I nodded. Libby stood up and plodded to the front of the class, her mouth turned down and still looking cross. I thought about how to do an "A," then knelt down and motioned for Libby to do the same. She looked confused, but she did it, about two feet away from me. Then I grabbed Libby's hands and pulled her toward me slowly, and I pushed my head forward until my forehead touched hers, still holding onto her hands. The kids laughed and clapped.

"Well done, Libby and Camile!" Miss Calista said. "That was very creative. Now that's what I want from all of you," she said to the class.

Libby and I went back to our seats. Libby wasn't mad anymore, she was grinning now. She laughed as the other kids did their letters, sometimes one person, sometimes two, depending on the letter. When everyone in the class had had a turn, Miss Calista said we had to finish the alphabet.

"Do I have any volunteers?"

"Hey, let's go do 'W'!" Libby said. She grabbed my hand and dragged me up to the front. It was exciting to have someone holding my hand like that. I told Libby to sit on the floor so we were facing each other with our legs out.

"Do what I do," I whispered. I leaned back on my arms and she copied me, then I put my feet together and stuck them straight out and up, toward Libby, and balancing on my butt. She copied me and rested her heels against mine up in the air.

"Very good again, girls," Miss Calista said. " 'W' is a hard letter to make."

At lunchtime I went to sit with Libby, but she was already sitting with Gigi and Nancy, and ignored me. I didn't mind because I was starting to figure out how people made friends. Now all I had to do was figure out what to talk about.

CHAPTER 21
DRAWING MERMAIDS

The summer school art class got me started in drawing, and I taught myself how to draw mermaids from the book I got out of the library. It showed me how to put circles and triangles together to make a mermaid shape, then you add the details and paint them if you want. Of course, my mermaids didn't look anything like Mermary, and she didn't know what they were when I first showed them to her.

After a while I didn't need the book anymore, I could draw a mermaid from memory. My mother saw the drawings.

"Nice, Camile," she said. "Did you learn this in your art class?"

I shook my head and showed her the book from the library. "But they don't look like these mermaid drawings." On the cover of the book were three beautiful mermaids with long hair and harps.

"Cammie, the people who draw these went to school for years to study art. They drew for thousands and thousands of hours to get good enough to be published in a book."

She brought tracing paper home the next day. "If you trace the mermaids, you might get a feel for how to draw them more realistically."

So I started tracing the mermaids in books. Even the tracings didn't look like much like the drawings until I got good at it. After a while I traced pictures of other sea creatures as well, like fish and octopi and sea horses.

I took some of my drawings and tracings to school one day and showed them to my art teacher after class. First she looked at the ones I drew with circles and triangles.

"Cute!" she said. "I love the way you painted them, the watercolors go out of the lines and look watery."

I hadn't done it on purpose, I just had a big brush so I couldn't keep inside the lines very well.

"I'm glad you're practicing drawing at home," she said. "Have you tried copying the mermaids free-hand?"

I knew that meant drawing without tracing paper. I shook my head.

"Give it a try, just to see what you can do," she said. "Something else you can try, is tracing the basic shape of the mermaid, then add features like the hair, or their eyes and mouth and nose without tracing them. And you can try making up the background instead of copying what you see in the book. It will develop your art imagination."

After my check-in with Mermary, when she went into her rest state and was curled up in her shell, I traced a mermaid outline from one of my books, then filled it in free-hand, trying to copy the picture in the book, but I didn't like it. I showed it to my mother when she got home.

"It's all right Camile," she said. "This is just a first try. Keep doing it, and you'll find your own way. And don't compare your work to the pictures in the books because you might get discouraged."

So I tried it again. I traced the basic mermaid shape, then closed the book. I drew in scales and fins, and gave her big eyes and a smile, and I put a pearl necklace on her. Then I made up the background to be a mermaid's house. It looked like a human house, so I drew furniture like a mermaid would have, with a mirror vanity and shell decorations. I drew a big shell for her bed with a pillowy mattress.

When I was done I drew it again, this time without tracing. I thought the house still looked too human, so I drew fish coming in through the windows like birds so it would look like it was supposed to be underwater. Then I made a cat-fish, only I made the top half a cat, and the bottom half a fish. And instead of house plants, I drew a sea-flower growing from the sand. When I used my imagination I liked my drawings better.

I tried drawing Mermary when she was swimming, with the fins where they were supposed to be on her back and arms. It didn't look like her, but at least you could tell it was a mermaid, and it was really fun drawing her. Plus, the drawings got better the more I drew.

The next week I took my drawings to school to show my art teacher, and she showed them to the whole class.

"Maybe you'll be an illustrator when you grow up, Camile," she said.

CHAPTER 22
AN INVITATION

The end of summer school was coming up. After that, there would be two weeks before school started, which would be the last week of August. I still sat next to Libby sometimes, but once she asked me crossly why I never talked, and another time told me to stop stalking her, so I didn't for a few days. Then on Monday, the last week of summer school, I sat next to her again in writing class.

Libby looked at me and I blurted out, "Want to come over?"

Libby stared at me and I was afraid she was going to say I was stalking her again. But instead she said, "What?"

"Do you want to come over?"

"You mean, to your house?"

I nodded. I had asked my mother already, and she said to invite Libby for Tuesday, so she would have time to ask her parents for permission. She said she'd leave work early so she could meet my friend. She got chocolate chip cookies for us. She acted more excited about it than me.

"My mother said I could invite you."

"You asked your mother if I could come over?"

I nodded, then I said yes, remembering Libby had gotten after me for not talking.

"When?" Libby asked.

"Tomorrow? Ask your parents tonight."

"Okay!"

The next morning while everyone was getting seats for movement class, Libby came over to me. Her hair was in a ponytail, and she was wearing a yellow T-shirt and red overalls that looked newish. Even her glasses looked clean.

"Hi, Camile," she said.

"Hi."

"Hey, I brought something for you." She put her hand in her pocket and brought out a yellow-and-black butterfly pin, sort of like a monarch.

"Thank you, Libby." I pinned it to my T-shirt. The pin was a little bent, so she helped me.

"Are we still going to your house after school?" she asked. Her voice sounded funny, kind of wobbly, not her normal loud voice, like she was afraid I'd changed my mind. I nodded.

"Are we going to take a shuttle?"

I nodded again, and Libby grinned. She didn't seem so bad when she smiled.

Libby was really nice to me that day. She sat next to me for each class, and in the cafeteria brought me over to where Nancy and Gigi were sitting, but they didn't seem to mind because we sat opposite them.

"Hey, you guys," Libby said.

"Hey, Libby," Gigi said.

"Hi, Camile," Nancy said.

"What are you guys going to do for the rest of the summer?" Libby asked them while we were eating.

I thought I saw Nancy poke Gigi with her elbow.

"Nothing much," Gigi said. "How about you?"

"Oh, babysit my little brothers. Today I'm going over to Camile's house."

"Good," Gigi said.

"Where do you live, Camile?" Nancy said.

"A block from the beach," I said. Then I remembered what my mother told me about making conversation. If someone asked you a question, ask them a question back, even if it was the same thing. "Where do you live?"

Nancy and Gigi looked at each other, then at Libby.

"Over near the mall," Gigi said.

I looked at Nancy, but she didn't answer the question. Instead, she asked, "What's your favorite class in summer school?"

"Movement," I said. I unwrapped my cookie, then put it down. "How about you?"

"I like writing. Mr. Mildigger makes it seem so easy."

"I like Green Jerry's class," Libby said. "He's so funny."

I was surprised. I thought Libby hated that class because she tried not to do anything, and Green Jerry was usually too busy to notice. But maybe that's why she liked it.

Libby hung around me all during his class. She even did everything Green Jerry asked her to do, as long as it was the same thing I was doing. We were putting the compost we made on all the plants around the community center. Libby stuck by me like she thought I would leave her behind or something.

When we got on the shuttle after school, I heard someone say, "Oh no, there's Libby." It was a guy at the back of the bus. "Why is she taking the shuttle?"

"Hey, Libby, get off the bus," his friend said. "You live right around the corner."

"I'm going over my friend's house, so there," she said. We got a seat together and sat down.

"She's with that psycho girl," I heard his friend said. "What a team."

People said I was shy and never talked, but I never heard anyone say I was psycho. I knew it meant a bad kind of crazy. I just ignored them, but Libby turned around and glared at them.

"You guys better shut up," she said. "I'll go back there and kick your butts." She looked like she was actually going to do it.

"Hey, no fighting on my bus," the driver said, standing up. "Take it outside."

"Ooooo, I'm sca-a-a-red," the first guy said.

"You better be," Libby said.

I was afraid the bus driver was going to throw us all off the bus, but Libby turned around. We heard the guys giggle and mumble something we couldn't hear, but Libby ignored them.

"What's your favorite TV show?" she asked me.

"Sometimes I watch science and history channels, but mostly I don't watch TV."

"You don't?"

"No. When I was little I watched cartoons on the weekends. How about you?"

The shuttle was full and we took off.

"I still watch cartoons, but just with my brothers. They're still little. What do you do then, if you don't watch TV?"

"My homework. Or I read. Sometimes I draw."

"Oh, yeah. Can you show me how to draw mermaids?"

I nodded. After a while I pulled the ringer. "This is my stop," I told her.

As we got off the shuttle, the guys at the back said, "Whew, now we can breathe again!"

"Yeah, open the windows, man!"

Libby looked at them and I was afraid she was going to go back there and get in a fight with them, but she laughed and waved as if they were her friends. "See you in sixth grade, suckers!"

"Which one is your house?" she asked.

I pointed at our light green house one block away. "My mother will be home soon." We started walking.

"Your mom's not home?"

I shook my head. "Is that all right?" I had heard some kids say they couldn't go over someone's house if their parents weren't there.

"Yeah. Where is she?"

"At work."

"What does she do?"

I told her, but Libby didn't know what that was, so I explained it to her.

"Can we go down to the beach?"

"I'm not allowed. Anyway, this is my house." I pointed to the bungalow.

"That color makes your house look like it's cool inside," she said.

"It is," I said.

We went inside and Libby looked around at everything. "Wow, your house is nice, and it's so tidy! How do you get it to smell so good, like cinnamon?"

"My mother drinks cinnamon tea. She boils cinnamon sticks with a lot of water. She also puts a stick into her coffee. She says cinnamon helps her think," I said.

"Can we have some?" Libby asked.

I nodded. I went into the kitchen and plugged in the electric kettle, then got two cups ready with cinnamon tea bags in them. I couldn't make it the way my mother did unless she was home. Besides, that took a long time.

"Do you have your own room?" Libby asked. I nodded. "How many brothers and sisters do you have?"

"None. I'm an only child."

"Wow, you're so lucky. I have two little brothers and my mother's going to have another baby. Can I see your room?"

We went upstairs. I had told Mermary I was going to bring someone home so I knew she would be hiding.

"Wow," Libby said. "You have a really pretty room! Did you decorate it?" She wandered around, looking at the canopy bed with heart pillows and my stuffed animals and pink-and-white striped walls.

"Me and my mom did," I said. "I mean, my mom and I did. What's your room like?"

"Oh," Libby said, her smile going away. "It's kind of small. It has old brown wall paper with tiny flowers on it. The ceiling is slanted, and it's really hot in the summer and cold in the winter." She saw the aquarium.

"Hey, you have goldfish!" She got up close and looked in. "They're really pretty. What are their names?"

"Actually, they're guppies," I said. "The one with the zebra tail is Buckaroo, and the orange-and-blue one is Orange-Gina."

She opened the lid. "Hey, why do you have a block of wood in here?"

"Oh, sometimes I put my dolls on that and play mermaid." I was getting nervous, even though I couldn't even see Mermary.

"Really? Do you have mermaid dolls?" she asked.

"Only one." I brought all my dolls out and lined them up in front of the tank with the little basket of clothes next to them. Libby picked up the mermaid doll and turned her from side to side. Then she put a little plastic crown on her head, and then tried to put Mermary's mirror in her hand. Finally she put it down and looked at the other ones.

"What are your dolls' names?"

I told her. Libby picked up each one and touched their clothes and their little shoes. "They're so cute! I love all their little clothes."

All the while I kept looking past Libby at the tank. Once I noticed Mermary peeking at Libby around the wide leaf of a water plant.

"How many dolls do you have?" I asked.

"One that's missing its arms. My brother pulled them out. I have another that I found in a lot near my house, but it doesn't have any clothes. And I have a sock monkey my grandmother made. I sleep with him."

I heard my mother's car pull into the driveway.

"My mom's home. Let's go downstairs so I can introduce you."

"Okay."

Libby went out and I turned back to look at Mermary and wave. My mother came in and put her bag and papers down. Libby had her hands in her pockets and stood quietly until I introduced them.

"Nice to meet you, Libby. Is that short for Elizabeth?"

"Yes, but only my grandfather calls me that."

"What do you like to be called?"

"Elizabeth. Libby's okay too." She smiled.

My mother went into the kitchen. "You haven't had your cookies yet, girls. Why don't you sit down at the table and I'll bring you your tea." She took the cookies out of the box and put them on a plate for us and gave us napkins. She also brought over a bowl of fruit. I took a tangerine and started peeling it.

"What's that?"

"A tangerine. I'll split it with you."

"It smells good."

My mother sat down with us and asked Libby questions, like where she lived and how many were in her family, and what her mother and father did. Her mother stayed home and her father worked at the Hazardous Waste facility outside of town. Libby was on her very best behavior and said "please" and "thank you." She was actually really nice, and I wondered why she didn't act like that all the time.

"I got to go to summer school because I got a special scholarship," she told my mom.

"Why that's wonderful, Elizabeth. You must be really smart."

Her smile went away again, but she didn't say anything. After we had cookies, my mother went to work at her computer. I got out my paper, pencils, and crayons and showed Libby how to draw mermaids. We drew and colored for a while.

"I better get home," Libby said. She seemed sad.

"Would you like to stay for dinner?" my mother asked.

"No, I better not."

I put down my crayons. "Should we call your mother?"

"Oh, she doesn't have a car. I can walk," Libby said.

"Oh no, I wouldn't think of it," my mother said. "I'll take you. This way I can meet your mother too."

Libby seemed uncomfortable about this, but she didn't say anything. She sat in the front seat and I sat in back. She was quiet on the way to her house except to give my mother directions. Her house looked small, and there were dry weeds in the yard, and an old wooden fence with broken slats. We pulled up and I saw a woman with a big stomach sitting on the porch and two little boys in the yard. She saw us and frowned.

"Where have you been, Libby? You were supposed to be home hours ago."

"Oh, Elizabeth," my mother said. "Didn't you ask for permission to come over?"

"I forgot," Libby said. My mother got out of the car, and Libby turned around and whispered, "She wouldn't have let me."

"Hello," my mom said. "I'm Inez, and this is my daughter, Camile. We had Libby over today. I didn't know she didn't have permission."

"Hello Inez and Camile," she said. "Glad to meet you." She didn't sound glad. "Libby is supposed to tell me where she's going to be. She has chores." She glared at Libby. "You better get in there."

Libby waved at me. "'Bye, Camile, I had a really nice time today. Thank you, Inez."

"You know better than to call grown-ups by their first name," Libby's mom said.

"Oh, yeah. Thank you, Mrs. Barcela." She picked up the smaller boy and took the other one by the hand and went inside.

"Next time ask *me* if you want to play with Libby," Camile's mother told me. "My daughter forgets these things. I was worried."

"I'm sorry," I said. "I will." My mother apologized too.

Libby hung out at school with me for the rest of that week, but I didn't think to ask for her phone number. My mother drove me over to her house one day after summer school was over. Libby's mother answered the door.

"Hello, Mrs. Jones," I said. "Can Libby come over for a play date?"

"No," Libby's mother said. "She has to stay here today."

I was really disappointed.

"You can come over sometime and play here if you want," Mrs. Jones said.

I wrote down my phone number and gave it to her, but Libby never called me.

CHAPTER 23
A BIG PROBLEM

I never got tired of being with Mermary, of watching her swim, of playing with her, either with dolls or dancing with her, or even telling her everything I learned at school. The problem was, Mermary was growing. Some people on aquarium sites on the Internet said pet fish grew in proportion to the size tank they were in, but it was starting to seem like Mermary might be getting too big for the tank. She was longer and bigger around now, and I could see her features clearly when I went into my room. I didn't know what to do about it. I could ask for a bigger tank, but my mother would wonder why I needed one. Several times she asked me why I didn't get more fish. I told her I liked the fish I had. Finally she brought home a couple of goldfish, one was orange and the other was a fat one that was orangey-red and white.

She came into my room when I went to float the bag in the aquarium. The first thing she saw when I opened the aquarium was Mermary's raft. She frowned.

"Why do you have a piece of wood in here?"

"Sometimes I put my mermaid doll on it," I told her.

Sea-li and some of my other dolls were sitting on the desk next to the aquarium. I had forgotten to put them away after the last time we played dolls. I put them away now. My mother checked everything, the water, the temperature, the sand at the bottom. Everything was clean because Mermary always let me know when it was time to change the water, but I was still worried she would see the mermaid.

"You're doing a good job of keeping the tank clean, Cammie," she told me. "I'm proud of you."

The whole time, Mermary hid in the midst of the seaweed. She had a trick now where she held on to the stem of a water plant in the middle of the seaweed forest and let her tail float upward, as if she was a plant too, then stayed really still until the person left. It was probably one of the ways mermaids stay hidden in the ocean when there were humans around.

My mother stared into the tank for a long time, turning her head. I couldn't tell what she was looking at, and I hoped she wasn't looking at Mermary and wondering what she was. I held my breath.

"Okay," she finally said. "Leave the fish in the bag until the water is the same temperature as the aquarium, then you can let them out."

I left the room with my mother, in case Mermary started begging me to let the fish out and my mother heard. Later I came back, and Mermary was trying to tear the bag open.

"Here, let me get that," I said.

I undid the tie. Mermary reached in and shooed the fish out, then chased them around the tank. I laughed, watching her. The goldfish were small, and a perfect addition to the tank. But a few days later Mermary told me the aquarium was starting to feel too small. That was what I'd been afraid of, and why I hadn't wanted any more fish.

"I need more room to swim," she told me. "Do you think I could go back out to that basin I used to live in? You could fill it to the top with water and put all these plants in there."

I didn't think it was a good idea to put her back into the drain's basin.

"I don't think it'll be safe, Mermary," I said.

"Is there another place I can go?"

When I first adopted her, I didn't think about what would happen when she grew big. Now I realized Mermary couldn't live in the aquarium forever.

"What about the ocean?" she asked.

"The ocean? But . . . it's too big. Something could eat you." But obviously, mermaids managed to survive in the ocean. "I'll think of something," I promised her.

I had to do something for Mermary, but what? I couldn't bear the thought of putting her in the ocean where I might never see her again. On the other hand, the way she was growing, I wouldn't be able to keep her a secret from my parents much longer either. What I was really afraid of was her going away from me. I didn't know what to do.

CHAPTER 24
THE SOLUTION

Summer was getting close to ending. I'd had so much fun I hated for it to be over, but I was looking forward to being in the sixth grade too. School would be starting in two weeks. My mother took me to school to register, pay tuition, and get a new uniform. I was growing too.

While my mother was taking care of school business, I went out to the school yard and sat on a bench. It faced Lake Meredith. The citizens of Luna Beach were very proud of our lake. We kept it clean, and there was a bird sanctuary with three little islands not far from the opposite shore, where birds roosted and no one was allowed to bother them. There were also turtles. My mother had told me they were non-native, and they were there because some kids had probably set their pet turtles free in the lake when they didn't want them anymore. I could see them sometimes, sunning themselves on rocks in the shallow parts of the lake.

All of a sudden I wondered if Mermary could live in the lake. I had read stories about mermaids who did, so why not Mermary? She would have lots of room to swim, and there were little fish she could eat. It was across the street from Our Lady of the Lake school, so she would still be close to me. When I got home I talked to her about it.

"Is the lake a lot bigger than the drain's basin?"

"Oh yes, lots bigger."

"Is it as big as your whole room?"

"It's more than ten times bigger."

"Is it as big as that?" She pointed to the ocean.

"No, but the lake should be big enough for you, no matter what size you get. What do you think about that?"

"Wonderful!" She clapped her hands and did somersaults in the water before surfacing again. "Will the fish go with me?"

"No, they probably wouldn't be safe in the lake. A bird or a big fish could eat them when you weren't looking. Anyway, there will be lots of fish in the lake."

Mermary didn't seem to mind. She was excited, but I was sad. I wouldn't get to talk to her all the time, or play dolls with her. But I didn't want Mermary to know I was sad.

Later I cheered up a little. It wasn't as if she was going into the ocean where, who knows when I'd see her again.

CHAPTER 25
FIRST DAY OF SCHOOL

During the last two weeks of summer I thought about how I was going to get Mermary from the house to the lake without my mother knowing what I was doing. She would never believe I was taking my fish in for a show and tell; that was for kindergartners.

Then, the night before the first day my mother said, "Cammie, I have to go into work much earlier than usual this week. If you got up earlier, I could drop you by school, but what will you do until the school opens?"

I thought about it. "I can take the bus. I know how. I did it all summer." I held my breath while I waited to see what my mother thought about this.

"All right. I can pick you up after school."

The next morning my mother woke me up before she left for work.

"Cammie, it's time to get up and get ready for school. I've left your bus fare on the table, next to your lunch box. Should I pick you up at school or the library?"

"Library, please."

As soon as my mother went out and closed the door, I got up and went over to Mermary. She was zipping through the water as fast as she could go, excited that today she was going to live in her new home. She paused in her zipping to kiss me good morning through the glass, then I went to wash up and put on my uniform.

I skipped breakfast so I would have plenty of time to walk to school and release Mermary. I grabbed my plastic beach bucket from the basement and ran up to my room. I took the whole lid off the aquarium. Mermary immediately surfaced.

"Hi, Mermary, are you ready?"

"Yes!"

"Okay, let me put some water in the bucket before you get in. You can help me by keeping the fish away." She dove back in and herded the fish to the bottom of the tank. I put in some plants too. If someone looked into the bucket, Mermary would have something to hide in.

"Now I have to put you in the bucket," I said. I cupped my hands and she jumped into them. It was always so exciting to hold Mermary. I kissed her little wet head and put her in the bucket. She immediately started scrabbling against the sides, but she couldn't climb them. I knew she didn't like being confined or not being able to see.

"You won't be able to see anything until we get to the lake," I told her. "It won't be too long, then you'll see much more than ever. Can you wait?"

"Yes," she said, and settled down.

I tested the bucket to see how heavy it was. I knew from cleaning the aquarium that water is really heavy, that was why I didn't put very much in. Luckily Mermary wasn't too heavy, and she didn't need too much water.

I put on my knapsack, then picked up my lunch box in one hand and the pail on my way out the door, and set out walking to school. It was a beautiful day and I wished the pail was clear so Mermary could see out. But she could see trees and telephone poles overhead, and she asked about them.

"Those are tree branches. They probably look different because you're walking underneath them, instead of looking out at them," I told her.

It was just before eight by the time I got to school. School started at eight-thirty. Lakeside Drive ran all around the lake. I stood at the crosswalk to wait until the crossing guard blew her whistle so that the children who lived on that side of the lake could cross to school. I was the only one going in the other direction, but kids were talking and didn't pay any attention to me. The only one who looked at me was the crossing guard, but she didn't say anything.

Near to my school was a colonnade with a climbing vine growing over it. From the center were steps down to a concrete platform over the water where people probably once launched boats, but now used to feed the ducks or go fishing. A fountain sprayed upward in that part of the lake, a little way away from the landing. Mermary could smell the water and was jumping up the side of the bucket, anxious to get out. So I sat down at the edge of the platform and lifted her up out of the bucket.

"See how big the lake is?"

"Wow," she said. "It's huge!"

I kissed her on the head and held her out over the water. She dove in and then surfaced.

"I love it!" she said. She looked all around, then pointed at the church.

"What's that?"

"That's a church." I pointed at my school that was across the courtyard from it. "And that's my school."

"'Lady of the Lake,'" she said, remembering the name. "*I'm* the lady of the lake now."

I laughed. "You're the lady of *this* lake," I said. "The Virgin Mary is the Lady of all the lakes in the world." I had told her the basics of the Catholic religion when she first came inside to live with me. I had even baptized her, although I hoped that wouldn't send her to Catholic heaven instead of mermaid heaven in the moon. I watched her swim and play around in the fountain, and was glad she was so happy. Finally the early bell rang, which meant I had ten minutes before class started.

"Mermary, please be careful and keep out of sight so no one will see you."

"Okay, but why?"

"Because if the grown-ups find out about you, they might take you away, and they'll never bring you back. It's not just my mother. It's probably any grown-up."

"Why would they do that?"

"That's just what humans do. You know how you're curious and ask questions? People are like that too. Unfortunately, some people don't have good intentions." I looked at her. She nodded. "Now I have to go. 'Bye now."

I was trying not to cry. Mermary leapt and sailed through the air and dove, then did that several times in a row.

"And make sure you don't do that when people are around, okay?"

"Okay," she promised.

I hoped putting her in the lake had been the right thing to do.

"Don't be sad, Cammie," Mermary said. "I know I'll be happy here."

I didn't realize she could tell I was sad. I smiled and told her I would come back after school to see her. Thinking about that made me feel a lot better.

"A bell will ring in the afternoon. That's the three o'clock bell, and it means school is over. I'll come over to see you before I meet my mother at the library—" I pointed at the library, which was across from the colonnade and one street.

I was crying on the way back to school. There were a couple of other kids crossing too. The guard noticed.

"Are you okay, little girl?" she asked.

I wiped my eyes and nodded. Once I got across the street, I went into the church, to the white statue of Our Lady of the Lake. I said a prayer and asked Mary to keep my mermaid safe.

CHAPTER 26
THE MERMAID'S FIRST DAY

The fifth grade classroom windows faced the lake, and all that first day I kept looking out the window, even though I couldn't see my little mermaid from that distance. I worried whether she was okay, if the lake was too cold for her, if she would get lonely, and a dozen other things.

Our teacher was a nun this year, Sister Marie Anthony. The nuns who taught in our school were sisters of the Holy Names. My mother told me that nuns used to wear habits with veils, but now they dressed like everyone else. Although my parents weren't very religious, they sent me to Lady of the Lake School because they said I would get a very good education, and it wasn't far from our house.

Also, there were no bullies because we had a "zero-tolerance for bullying policy." Actually, a couple of the kids *were* bullies, just not at school. I'd seen bullying a couple of times on my way home from school. No one ever bullied me though, probably because I was so quiet.

Most of the same girls and boys who I started first grade with were still in my class. I thought about what Mermary had told me about how to make friends. She had said, "You just start talking to them, like you did with me." So on the first day of class, I turned around and smiled at the girl behind me. Her name was Bambi. She smiled back. I was surprised, and it made me feel happy. I had always been too shy even to look at people, but it seemed a little easier now. Maybe it was because I was older. Or maybe because I had practice now, with Mermary.

The school books we were going to use were already in our desks, and Sister Marie Anthony had us take them out, put our names in them, and look at them. She told us how our curriculum was changing from fourth grade, how she was going to teach, and said we were going to start getting serious about homework—as if we had been playing around in the lower grades. She also had us take some aptitude tests in math and English and write some paragraphs on topics she announced because she wanted to see what our writing skills were. It was an easy day and it would have been fun if I hadn't been so worried about Mermary.

As soon as school was over, I went back across the street to see Mermary. I looked to make sure no one was around before I called her. There were kids walking under the colonnade on their way home, but mostly they didn't pay any attention to me. I sat down on the edge like I had that morning and called her. I was so relieved when she came up smiling.

"How was your first day in the lake?" I asked.

"I loved it! I swam as far as that tree," she pointed to a tree at a point that curved into the lake, "and then I swam all around this area. There's no sand at the bottom of the lake, like at home."

I liked that Mermary called the aquarium home.

"What is at the bottom?" I asked.

"This dark, soft stuff, like what I had at the bottom of the basin, only more. Lots more."

"Mud?"

"Yes, mud," Mermary said. "And there are all kinds of things to see in it."

"Like what?"

"Bottles and cans, cups, lots of things I don't know the name of, like a long stick thing with plastic string attached and a sharp hook at the end—"

"That sounds like a fishing pole."

"—and one of those." Mermary pointed to an old man on the lake in a small boat. "Only it's broken and on its side."

"That's a row boat," I told her.

"A row boat," she repeated. "And there's some of those things he's using to move the boat."

"Those are oars."

"Some were wooden and rotten. Some are metal."

Now Mermary was telling me about *her* day, the way I used to tell her when I came home from school.

"How was school?" she asked, almost as if she'd read my mind.

"My teacher's name is Sister Marie Anthony. I like her, even though I think she's strict. The books are bigger and the math and English will be a lot more complicated this year," I told her. "Also, Sister talked to us about public speaking. Sister Marie said 'part of public speaking is presenting yourself to people. You should always stand straight and project your voice.'" I changed my voice to sort of like Sister's, and Mermary laughed. "'Every time I call on you in class is an opportunity to practice your speaking skills. For homework you will develop what you wrote in class.'" I wasn't really making fun of Sister Marie, although I was exaggerating because Mermary thought it was funny.

"Did you write about me?"

"Of course not, silly mermaid, although I wanted to. I wrote about summer school, since my family doesn't take a vacation until winter." I didn't tell Mermary how worried I'd been about her. I looked at my Little Mermaid watch.

"I better go. My mom's going to pick me up at the library, and she'll start looking for me if I'm not there." I pointed across the street to where the library was.

"Okay," Mermary said. "Goodbye, Cammie."

I blew her a kiss, and she copied me. She didn't seem sad that I was leaving, but then, she never had. A mermaid in one of the movies I'd seen said that mer-people didn't believe in love. I wondered if that could be true.

All of a sudden I blurted, "Mermary, do you love me?"

But Mermary was already gone.

CHAPTER 27
PUBLIC SPEAKING

The day after we turned in our homework, Sister read and corrected them, then had us do yet another rewrite.

On Friday that week, she said, "I have been enjoying watching you develop and improve your essays. Now I think your classmates will like hearing what you did over the summer. Remember on the first day of school, I talked to you about public speaking. You should stand straight and project your voice. I'm going to have each one of you come up to the front and read your work to the rest of the class."

My heart sank. In the lower grades everyone had to stand up and read aloud so the teacher could check our reading skills. I always hated it. During summer school I had gotten up in front of the class a lot for dance, but mostly I didn't have to say anything. I couldn't listen to the first kids who read because I was so scared. My turn came, and I stood up in front and held my essay in front of my face. I tried to read but nothing came out of my mouth.

"Camile," Sister Marie said. "Hold the page down so we can see your face. Now take a deep breath, and try to relax."

I did what she said, but I couldn't relax, and I couldn't read. I felt tears coming to my eyes, but I didn't want to cry in front of the whole class. I looked out the window at the lake, and thought of Mermary, and how I used to read to her, no problem. It seemed like I got a little calmer. I took another breath and started reading. It wasn't so bad. Thinking about Mermary had helped!

After I read, I was able to listen better to everyone else. One girl wrote about going on a road trip to Mexico to visit family and she was surprised that most of the people they met spoke English. Another girl went to Yellowstone Park and saw the geysers spout off. One boy wrote about going to the moon on a spaceship he and a scientist friend had built, and all there was to eat was green cheese and water.

"Michael felt he had a dull summer, so he developed this story from a dream he had," Sister said. "It was a very imaginative way of completing this assignment."

I was disappointed I hadn't written about Mermary after all. Sister would just have said the same thing about my paper, since most people thought mermaids weren't real.

CHAPTER 28
MERMAID IN THE LAKE

I went to visit Mermary every school day in the morning, and again in the afternoon before I went home. I missed not being able to spend a lot of time with her like I did over the summer, and I pined for her on the weekends. But in another way, I liked it. It was kind of an adventure to visit her in a natural environment, and having a real mermaid as a friend.

Now that she was living in a lake, it seemed like Mermary was growing really fast. She was almost as long as my forearm, and she was filling out more. I had put her in the lake just in time. Also, her skin was changing. In the aquarium she was a shade of green, to match the seaweed plants in there. Now her top half was darker, turning into the color of the lake, which was a greeny-brown, so it made it harder to see her. Her stomach was her normal color, only maybe lighter. I wrote down these changes in my mermaid journal when I got home.

After school, Mermary and I met at a point where there was a tree because I wasn't as visible there as at the landing by the colonnade. We started calling it Dragon Tree Point. It was actually a Tea Tree. I knew that because somewhere a sign said that was what they were, and they grew all around the lake. Tea trees didn't grow straight up and down like most trees. Their length grew long, along the ground, and twisted back and curved around, and they had a thick, rough bark that made it look like a dragon. I would sit inside the trunk of the tree at Dragon Tree Point, and be sort of hidden. From there Mermary could see in both directions if someone was coming.

We agreed on hand signals. I had learned some sign language in kindergarten, so "follow me" is putting up your thumbs and motioning to the right. But I modified it to only one hand so it wouldn't be so obvious. If I crossed my hands flat in front of me and scissored them, it meant not to come out. If I put two fingers and a thumb and "quacked" them, it meant duck, not the bird, but to go underwater. But I almost never had to use that one, it turned out Mermary had a good instinct about anyone coming near us. She would instantly duck if something unexpected happened, like a bird landing in the water, or someone passing behind me who I hadn't noticed, like a runner did once. She barely even made a splash. I would be talking to her, and all of a sudden she'd be gone. All I would see was a quick, underwater flash of her iridescent tail.

Mermary was exploring more and more of the lake. She told me where the deepest parts were, and where the shallows were. She told me that the bird refuge was fed by fresh water from a pipe. She hated motorboats and stayed away from them, but thought it was fun to swim under row boats and gondolas—people could rent gondolas on Lake Meredith—and listen to what people talked about.

"A woman was mad at her husband because he had gone out with another lady," Mermary told me. "He said, 'I told you she was just a friend,' and his wife said, 'then why didn't you tell her you had a wife?' and he said, 'I forgot.' 'Oh, like you forgot to put your wedding ring back on?'" Mermary was giggling and swimming crazily in squiggles as she told me, which was what she did when she thought something was funny. "Is that what humans do to make up with people? Take them on a boat ride?"

"I think he was probably trying to make it romantic," I said.

"Make what romantic?"

"His apology," I said. "Mermary, it scares me when you swim with boats. What if they notice you?"

"Oh, I swim far enough under the water so they can't see me. I can still hear them perfectly well."

Of course I had known that Mermary could hear me through the water and even the glass of the aquarium. I was glad to hear she didn't get near the boats.

Mermary had a new pastime too. She rooted around in the mud at the bottom of the lake and found things, like old bottles that were beautiful colors once they were cleaned up, old coins, and an object that was rusted shut, which she asked me about. It looked like an old pocket watch, but when I pried the cover open I saw it was a waterlogged compass.

I still brought her food. I always saved some of my tuna sandwiches because that was her favorite, but she was mostly eating fish that she caught now, and greenery that she gathered from the lake. She also ate eggs that she took from the nests of birds that had built their nests on the ground. Mermary had discovered she could wriggle up on the islands where the birds lived. She told me she went up on the lake side of the tiny islands so people couldn't see her from the shore. Maybe it was her new diet that was making her grow so fast.

Something else Mermary told me was that she liked eating food that people threw into the lake. When she described it, I knew it was mostly junk food: French fries, the remainder of hamburgers, onion rings, hot dogs. Once she even found a milkshake floating in the water.

"It was pink and it was really yummy!" she told me. "But I ate too much and threw up."

I never knew mermaids could throw up, but of course, if she was related to humans as I suspected, she probably did all the normal things that humans do, like vomiting. Something else to put into my notebook, which was now up to forty pages.

I couldn't spend a lot of time with Mermary anymore. I could only visit for ten minutes in the morning, and fifteen minutes or so after school. Once or twice I had been late getting to the library when my mother came to pick me up, and she wondered where I was. She didn't like that I was hanging around at the lake, she thought it might be dangerous. Of course I kept going to the lake after that, but I had to be very careful on the days she came to pick me up, and cut my time with Mermary even shorter.

Mermary was becoming very independent and didn't seem to mind. Still, she thought of me, because she always had stories to tell me, and sometimes gifts. Once she gave me an old silver ID bracelet with someone's name engraved on it. She always blew kisses to me when I showed up, and again when I left. We called them wind kisses.

CHAPTER 29
COSTUME

In September I told my mother I wanted to be a mermaid for Halloween. I had requested a book from the library on making mermaid costumes, so we read it together. There were about five different styles to choose from, and I picked out the one I wanted. The tail was form-fitting, and it had a fin that flared out sideways at the bottom and would hide my feet. The top was a bib and it had straps. My mom took my measurements and we wrote down how much fabric and other items we would need.

That Saturday we went downtown to buy them. At the fabric store we found some stretchy, shimmery blue-green fabric and a stiffer, plain green fabric for the fins and bib. We also got dark green hem tape for the veins on the fins, some elastic and green buttons. Then we went to a craft store, where I found a bag of shells that had holes drilled in them and a bag of pink iridescent sequins. My mother also took me to get green ballet-type shoes that I could wear under the fin, a green hair band, and a long-sleeved, light pink leotard to wear under the bib.

"You'll need to wear something underneath the costume because it'll be cold in late October. And it's better to wear pink instead of green, so the bib will stand out."

At home we spread out the fabric on the kitchen table, and following the guide in the book, my mother measured and then drew the outline of the fish body on the inside of the fabric, then cut it out. Next she cut out the fins and with a piece of chalk on the right side of the material, drew the veins. She helped me cut pieces of the hem tape to match the sizes of the ones my mother drew, then we pinned them in place. The hem tape had gluey stuff on the other side so they could be ironed in place, which she let me do. Then she ran the sewing machine down the middle of each one, even though the book didn't say to do it.

"The hem tape could become loose, especially after you walk around in it," my mom told me. "This will keep the veins on."

The seam made the veins look more realistic. My mother had learned sewing when she was young so she had ideas to add to the costume, like she scalloped the bottom of the fin, which made it really special.

I did whatever she told me to do to help, mostly ironing seams and hand-sewing. Before she sewed the bib part, she made a diamond pattern across the fabric with the sewing machine, then told me to sew sequins at each juncture. I also sewed sequins and shells to the waistband. Then I glued shells and glitter to the head band. It was so much fun to make, and it looked really pretty when we were all done. I put it on it and walked funny because it was narrow over the legs, but I didn't mind because it was like a mermaid swimming.

I put my costume on to show my father when he came home the following week.

"Whoa," he said when he saw me. "For a minute I thought my daughter had turned into a mermaid! Where did you get that?"

"Me and Mom made it for my Halloween costume."

"It was easy," my mother told him. "Cammie did the hard part, all the hand-sewing."

Of course, it was still ages before Halloween. I couldn't wait to show it to Mermary. I hadn't told her I was going to be a mermaid for Halloween, although I had told her about the holiday and what it was about. I wanted to surprise her.

CHAPTER 30
KNIVES

When Halloween was still a couple of weeks away, my mother and I went to a block sale near our neighborhood. That's when lots of people on the same block put out stuff they want to sell in their yard or driveway. It was a sunny day, but there was a cool breeze blowing and lots of leaves were falling from the trees and you could tell autumn was in full fall. My mother looked at books and old clothes, and sometimes kitchen tools. I looked at the books and toys.

At one house I found a really nice toy dagger in a sheath that was attached to a belt. It was gold and black, with a curved blade and a fancy handle with a scrolled end and red, green, and blue gems. A girl came over. She had short, curly, reddish hair and freckles. I recognized her from summer school.

"That's for a pirate costume. I was a pirate for Halloween last year," she said. "I'm going to be a ninja this year. What about you? Wait—don't tell me. You're going to be a mermaid, right?"

I smiled and nodded. She grinned.

"I remember you from summer school," she said. "You drew the mermaid pictures." Her name was Regina, although everyone called her Reggie. She was a tomboy. She usually sat at the back of class with two guys, Zander and Elmo, unless they were talking too much and the teacher separated them. "I liked your drawings, especially the way you drew them with three fingers, like in comic books."

I didn't know comic book characters only had three fingers because I never read them. She got a comic book from a pile she was selling.

"See?"

She showed me drawings of Donald Duck. I had seen him on TV but never noticed he only had three fingers and a thumb.

"Not all the comic book artists do that. Like Wonder Woman or Batman, those are drawn realistic style, so they have all five fingers."

Reggie talked a lot, but I didn't mind since I didn't say anything.

"Why don't you try on the dagger?"

I put it on. There was a mirror leaning up against the house, so I went over to look at myself. It was really nice, like something a queen would wear.

"Hey, why don't you wear that knife with your costume?" Reggie asked. "Mermaids should have knives, but they never do."

I was surprised. "They should?"

"How else are they supposed to get abalone off of rocks?" Reggie said. "What if she gets caught in a net? How are mermaids supposed to defend themselves?"

She was right. I remembered Mermary scrabbling at the plastic bag, trying to get out.

"What about sharks . . . or what if a scissor fish came after her?" All of a sudden Reggie grabbed some of my hair and pretended to cut it with her fingers, saying, "snip, snip, snip," making me giggle. Scissor fish were called that because their tail looks like an open pair of scissor, but I didn't mind being teased. No one except my parents had ever done that.

"If the mermaid had a knife, that scissor fish would be *her* next meal," Reggie said.

"How much?" I asked.

"Four dollars, and you can have all the comic books too."

I paid for it with my allowance money without asking my mother. I wasn't sure she'd let me buy it because she was against violence, and might think a knife was violent. Reggie gave me a paper bag with handles to put it all into. I thanked her and started to walk away, but then I came back. I stood there, staring at Reggie. She looked at me curiously.

"What?" she asked. "Change your mind?"

I shook my head. "T-trick-or-treating. Want to go with me?"

"I always go with Zander and Elmo," she said.

"Oh." I was disappointed. I started to leave.

"Wait, why don't you come with us? It'll be fun."

She got a pen and wrote down my phone number, and then wrote hers on my bag. I was so glad I had been able to ask, even though it had been really hard.

I caught up to my mother at the next house. I was thinking about Mermary. I didn't know if there was anything she needed to defend herself from in the lake, but I thought there might be mussels or clams, or plants she might need to cut. Down the street I found a tiny jackknife I thought would be the right size for Mermary. It was only fifty cents so I bought that too.

At home I put on my mermaid costume with the dagger. It looked really good. I couldn't wait for Halloween.

CHAPTER 31
TOPIC

Sister gave us an assignment to make another presentation to the class. I had hoped that last one would be it for the year, but no such luck. She passed out a list of topics and told us to either choose one, or come up with our own. Then we were supposed to write our ideas about it.

"Once you have a topic, I'll teach you how to write an outline, which you'll need for your presentation," she said.

One of the topics on the sheet was "The ocean, or anything related to the sea." I wrote down,

> Mermaids live in the ocean.
> There are lots of stories about mermaids.
> Are mermaids real?
> Mermaids are beautiful and magical.
> Other cultures believe in mermaids.

I wasn't sure if I had done it right. I looked around and saw that some of my classmates hardly had anything written down, but others were still writing. After a while, Sister said that if we had all written something, then to put our names on the paper and turn them in.

"But I only wrote one sentence," a boy named James said.

"That's all right," Sister said. "You'll be developing this idea. I can give you some ideas too."

When I got my topic back the next day, Sister had put a plus sign on it, which meant it was approved. At the bottom she wrote, "This can be a very interesting topic. Think about combining some of these ideas."

I read Mermary my list when I saw her that afternoon.

"I'm glad she approved my topic. I was afraid she was going to say it wasn't scientific."

"Can't mermaids be scientific?"

I laughed because that made me think of mermaids wearing white coats and looking through microscopes on the ocean floor. I knew Mermary meant the *topic* of mermaids could be scientific.

"Yes, but I can't talk about that, because then everyone would wonder how I knew all those facts about mermaids."

"Can't you say you read it in a book? Or online?"

"Well, the reason I've been reading all those books on mermaids was because I was trying to find factual information on them, but all I found were stories. Besides, if I said I read it someplace, people might want to read the same book, and they would find out I was lying. Or, at least, they would think I was."

"Why don't you talk about why mermaids are such a big mystery? Like why are there so many stories about mermaids, when people don't believe in them?"

"That's a good idea," I said. It was helping me to talk about my topic, making it clearer for me. "Anyway, it will be fun writing about it. The only thing I'm not looking forward to is the presentation itself."

"When is it?" Mermary asked.

"The week before Thanksgiving."

"Oh, well then on Thanksgiving, you'll be grateful that your presentation is over."

I laughed. "Yes, I will."

CHAPTER 32
A FRIEND AT LAST

I was excited to have someone to go trick-or-treating with. I always went with my parents, but the other kids I saw looked like they were having much more fun with each other. I was trying to be friendly with girls in my class, and they were being friendlier to me. But looking at them and smiling wasn't enough.

One Saturday morning my mother called me to the phone.

"Hey Camile, this is Reggie. Remember me?" It was the girl who sold me the pirate knife. She sounded excited. "I got some mermaid anime comic books for you. That's Japanese cartooning. Some of them have really cool art."

"How much?"

"You can just have them. Where do you live? I'll bring them over right now."

I gave her my address and told my mother she was coming over. I was excited, I'd never had anyone over! A few minutes later the doorbell rang. Reggie had ridden her bike over and brought it up onto our porch. She handed me four comic books.

"This is the best one," she said, pointing at the one on top. It had a drawing with a big-eyed mermaid in a river. "She's really smart, and brave too." Reggie looked past me into the house.

"Cammie, invite your friend inside," my mother called.

"Want to come in?"

"Yes!" She came in and looked all around. My mother came over to greet Reggie and I introduced them.

"It's nice of you to give your comic books to Camile," my mom said politely, although I knew she didn't really approve of them. She didn't think it was real literature. "Would you like some cookies and milk?"

"Sure! Thank you."

We sat at the table while my mother got us cookies and milk.

"How did you like the comic books?" Reggie asked. "Did you have any favorites?"

I nodded. "Cat Woman."

"Yeah, isn't she cool? She's my favorite too." Reggie seemed distracted. She kept turning her head to look around at the house.

"Do you have other favorites?" I asked.

"Yes, I've read some really old comic books about Wonder Woman. They're way cooler than the new ones, but the newer stories are more interesting." We talked about comic books while we ate our cookies. Reggie told me that she wanted to be a cartoon artist when she grew up, and that she already drew comic strips.

"I'll show them to you sometime." She leaned to see down a hallway. She finished her milk. "Hey, can I see your mermaid costume?"

Reggie was a very curious person. She looked into all the rooms as we went upstairs. She didn't make a big deal out of my room like Libby had, but made a beeline for the aquarium.

"You have fish, cool!" she said.

She got up really close and looked into it from the sides, and even went around to the back. She opened the lid. Of course, after Mermary left I took out her board because it wasn't fun to play mermaids without her.

"Why are there so many plants in there? You can't see the fish."

"So it's like a real ocean," I said.

"I used to have an aquarium," Reggie said. "Hey, I like the way you decorated the tank. It looks like a little bedroom. A little *mermaid* bedroom." I had left Mermary's shell bed with the plastic doll that didn't float in it, a little ceramic treasure chest, and her mirror stuck into the sand by the handle. She looked at me. "Like maybe you had a mermaid living in here once?"

It almost seemed like a question, but of course I didn't answer. If she only knew. It seemed like she was waiting for me to say something, but I didn't even shake my head. That would be somehow admitting it. Instead, I went and got out Sea-li and the other mermaid baby to show her.

"Sometimes I play mermaid dolls," I said. But Reggie somehow didn't seem the type to play with dolls.

"Are there any other aquariums in the house?" she asked.

I shook my head.

"Oh," Reggie said. She seemed disappointed. "Oh yeah, show me your costume."

I opened my closet door and brought it out.

"Wow," Reggie said. "That's the coolest mermaid costume I've ever seen! It looks great with that knife. Told ya. Where did you get the costume?"

"My mother and I made it."

"You *made* it?"

"Mostly my mother."

She turned it around to see the back. "Hey, I should be a pirate again this year, our costumes would be really great together! I can still wear my ninja costume to a Halloween party I'm going to."

Reggie asked if she could see the rest of the house. As I took her around it almost seemed as if she was looking for something. I remembered she had an old-looking house. Maybe that was why she was interested, because our house was newer.

"Can I see your backyard?" she asked.

I nodded and led her to the back yard. She stopped at the corner of the house where the open drain was.

"Hey, what's this?"

"Oh, that catches the rain from the gutters." She stooped down to look into it. It was starting to fill up again because there had been a few rainstorms. She picked up a stick and stirred it up. Finally she stood up and looked out toward the ocean.

"How far is the beach from here?"

"A block. Then there's the boardwalk."

"I have to go," she said suddenly. She headed toward the porch to get her bike. "I'll see you on Halloween. It's going to be really fun. Zander is going to be a skeleton, but Elmo doesn't know what he's going to be. He better decide soon, he likes to make his own costumes."

Reggie waved and took off in the direction of the beach. I was so excited about our Halloween plans, and especially to finally have a friend. I couldn't wait to tell Mermary.

CHAPTER 33
HALLOWEEN AT SCHOOL

Halloween fell on a Thursday. It was a cool, but sunny autumn morning. Everyone was wearing their costume to school. I was going to walk but my mother insisted on driving me.

"It'll take too long to walk to school because it's so form-fitting, you can't take regular steps," she said. She didn't mind about the knife, especially when I explained why a mermaid needed one.

She dropped me off in front of the church and I waved good-bye. As soon as I couldn't see her car anymore, I went to the street and crossed over to the lake. Everyone was staring at me, but then, all the children in costumes were being stared at. I realized I could hike up the bottom part of the costume and walk faster. I hurried over to the colonnade where I met Mermary every morning because it was closer than the Dragon Tree. Mermary surfaced. She was wearing a jagged half of a broken tennis ball on her head. One piece of it came down and wrapped around her chin and she peeked out between the tear.

"Mermary, why do you have that on your head?"

"Because it's Halloween. This is my costume! Do you like it?"

I said I did because she seemed so proud of it, and oftentimes I'd seen some people with really crazy costumes, so it wasn't really that strange.

"Your costume is really beautiful," Mermary said. "What are you?"

"A mermaid!"

"You *are*?"

I looked down at myself. It made sense that I didn't look like a mermaid to a *real* mermaid. "Well, that's what I'm *supposed* to be." I told her how my mother and I made it, and how I had bought the knife from Reggie.

"The material on the bottom half kind of looks like what fish wear," she said.

I laughed at the way she put it. "I know. That's why I chose it." The early bell rang across the street. I couldn't believe my time with Mermary was almost up.

"I walk slower in this costume so I better start back now. I probably won't be able to visit after school," I told her. "My mother's coming to pick me up and she said she was going to try to get here early."

"That's all right," Mermary said. "I'll see you tomorrow morning."

We blew each other wind kisses, and I headed back to school. A lot of my classmates were late, probably due to their costumes, so Sister allowed us time before class started to look at each other's costumes.

Some of the other kids had costumes they had bought, but a few had homemade ones. Karl Gladstone was a tree. He'd made his costume out of cardboard boxes that he'd cut open and taped together and painted. Tricia Lee came as an angel. Actually, she was supposed to be a statue of an angel, and her costume and make-up were all grey, whitish, and blackish. Two other girls had mermaid costumes too, Bambi and Kitty who were best friends. Kitty's costume was a shiny blue fabric decorated with tiny starfish, with a sort of tail gathered at the sides. Bambi's was light green and pink iridescent on the bottom with green plastic that was swept out to look like a tail fin, and a green sequin top. She had a wig on with long, bright red hair. I'd seen one like it at the super drugstore. They were both staring at me.

"Camile," Bambi said. "Your costume is totally awesome."

"Yeah," Kitty said. "Where did you get it?"

"My mother and I made it together."

"You made it?"

I nodded. "Your costumes are cute too," I said politely. "Did you make yours?" I asked Bambi.

"My mother did. I picked out the fabric."

"Hey, let's all walk together in the parade!" Kitty said.

"Yes, we'll be a contingent, like in regular parades," Bambi said. There was going to be a parade later, where everyone would show off their costumes to the rest of the school. "The Mermaid Contingent!"

I nodded. I couldn't believe they were inviting me to be with them. They also called me over to eat with them at lunchtime.

"We should start a mermaid club," Kitty said. "Anyone who loves mermaids can be in it."

"We could get mermaid tails and swim in your pool!" Bambi said. "You can get mermaid swimming suits on the Internet," she told me.

They were both looking at me like they were waiting for me to say something, so I nodded excitedly. Just like that, I had two new friends!

Mermaids were believed to be bad luck sometimes, but obviously they were good luck too.

It was hard to concentrate on school that day, probably because of the costumes and everyone thinking about trick-or-treating that night, but Sister made it fun for us. We had a spelling bee, and we got to watch a science movie on wolves. Then she read us a Halloween story about a witch who sometimes turned her cat into a person so she could discuss things with him, or go to human places together and cause mischief.

School let out early for the parade. The older kids, grades seven and eight, didn't get to wear costumes. They were going to vote on best costume, and were already in the school yard gathered at one end with their teachers. The first grade led the parade, marching in a line in front of everyone. Sometimes the audience clapped when they really liked someone's costume. The second graders went next and so on. When the school saw our Mermaid Contingent everyone clapped and cheered, and that made us giggle.

After school, Kitty's mother wanted to take pictures of us. "Let's go across the street so the lake will be in the background."

I was really glad she said that because I wanted Mermary to see the Mermaid Contingent and my new friends. We gathered by the side of the lake. No one was looking at the lake, and I looked quickly to see if Mermary was there. She put her face out of the water for a moment and winked at me, then quickly disappeared. Mrs. Connor got the idea to take more pictures under the colonnade, and then on the landing where the light was better.

"Pretend like you're going to dive into the lake," she said, and we posed, curving sideways with our hands over our heads.

My mother arrived and saw us by the lake. She parked and came over to talk to Mrs. Connor and meet my school mates. She was all smiles to see me with them.

"Can you come trick-or-treating with us?" Bambi asked, after the pictures.

"Yes, do!" Kitty said.

"Oh, I'm already going with someone," I said.

"Well, I don't see why that's a problem," my mother said, who wasn't going to let me pass up a chance to make friends. "Why don't you all go together?"

I said I would make sure it was okay, and Bambi and Kitty gave me their phone numbers.

"It seems like you're finally making some friends, Cammie!" my mother said on the way home. "How do you like it?"

I loved having friends, starting with Mermary, who had taught me how.

CHAPTER 34
HALLOWEEN NIGHT

I called Reggie to ask if it was okay that Bambi and Kitty wanted to come with us, and she thought it was cool that we all had mermaid costumes and said it was okay for them to come along.

"Be at my house about a half hour before sunset," she said. "My mom likes to take pictures."

My mom got on the Internet and checked the time of sunset, and I called Bambi and Kitty to tell them what time to come over. I wasn't hungry, but my mother made me eat dinner anyway.

"You're going to be eating lots of candy and who knows what else, so I want you to have a good meal in you before going out."

Mrs. Connor dropped off Bambi and Kitty. Bambi had on a cape that her mother made, and Kitty had on a white shawl because it was getting cool. I had my pink leotards on under the costume, so I wasn't cold.

My mom took us all over to Reggie's. She lived in a Victorian, and the front porch had been decorated with broken branches, autumn leaves, pumpkins, a big owl, and a really scary black cat, both fake. Everything was lit by little electric candles, so it all looked really spooky. Reggie's mother opened the door. The house had a spicy smell.

"Ahoy, mermaids!" Reggie said.

She wore a three-cornered hat and an eye patch, a lady's blouse with ruffles, and brown breeches tucked into black knee-hi boots. With it, she wore a wide belt with a musket stuck in the waist, and a cutlass. Her hair was tied back in a ponytail and she had drawn a curly mustache on her upper lip.

"Camile, introduce your friends," my mother said, so I said Bambi and Kitty's names, and Reggie introduced Zander and Elmo.

"And I'm Inez Barcela," my mother said, because I forgot to include her.

"I'm Jane, Reggie's mother," Reggie's mom said. She had short, curly hair, and she wore a black sweatshirt with orange writing that said, "YOU SAY 'WITCH' LIKE THAT'S BAD." "That's my husband, Joe," she said about the man in the front room, watching TV.

He looked over at us and waved. "Hi, kids. Hello, Inez."

Zander was a pirate too, except underneath the pirate costume he wore a skin-tight skeleton costume. He had a red kerchief on his head, a vest, brown cut-offs, and combat boots. His head mask wasn't on yet.

"I talked him into going as a pirate again," Reggie said.

"Yeah, I thought it would be even cooler to be a *skeleton* pirate."

At first I didn't know what Elmo was supposed to be. He had painted the top of his face green and wore a yellow-and-orange plastic beak. He had on a green sweatshirt with yellow feathers taped all along the arms and across the back, and green khaki pants rolled up to his knees. He was barefoot and his feet and legs were streaked and yellow. He also had green nail polish on his fingers and toes.

"Awk!" Elmo said, holding his arms out and moving his head side to side on his neck. "Pieces o' eight, pieces o' eight!" He flapped his arms.

"You're a parrot," Kitty said.

"A *pirate* parrot," he said.

The spicy smell in the house was hot apple cider that Reggie's mother served us. Reggie called it grog.

"That's what pirates used to drink when they were out to sea for a long time. It's a concoction of rum and lemon juice."

"I put lemon juice, orange slices, and lots of nutmeg in it so it tastes like rum," Reggie's mom told my mother. "There's no alcohol in it."

"Mo-om," Reggie complained. "You don't have to ruin it."

Reggie's mother winked at my mom. She picked up a camera.

"Okay, now everyone, pose!"

My mother got her phone out of her purse and they took pictures of us. Reggie stood between Kitty and me and put her arms around our shoulders. Zander stood behind Bambi and made his hands into claws over her head like he was going to grab her. Elmo got in front of all of us and stood on one foot with his arms spread out. He was the shortest one of us, plus he scrunched up and made himself even smaller to be more like a parrot.

Reggie thought we would be safe trick-or-treating because there were so many of us, but my mother insisted on going, and Reggie's mother decided to go too. Reggie and Zander groaned.

"We don't need chaperones," Reggie complained. "We're ten years old!"

"I'm responsible for my daughter and her friends," my mother said. "Nothing's going to happen to them on *my* watch."

"Don't worry," Reggie's mother said. "We'll hang back far enough so no one will know we're with you."

I didn't know why Reggie and Zander didn't want them to go. My mother and sometimes my father always went with me, plus I liked that she was going to be there.

We headed out, excited to show off our costumes and get candy. Lots of people had carved pumpkins and orange lights, or put giant spiders and webs on their houses. At one place, someone had stuffed pants and a shirt so it looked like a body leaning up against the house, with a skull for a head and an arrow stuck in his chest. Another place had a scarecrow in the yard with a lady's hat and six arms, made of sticks with gloves at the end. Some people had gone to a lot of work with their decorations, like making their front lawn into a graveyard with tombstones and bones sticking out of the ground here and there. Some even had scary music.

Whenever we went up on someone's porch, Elmo got up on one foot and hopped, pretending to be a parrot, Reggie would brandish her cutlass, and the three of us mermaids would put our arms on each other's shoulders. Zander would just roar, but it was hard to hear him because his voice was muffled behind the mask.

A couple of times we met other pirates. Once Reggie got into a sword fight.

"Avast there ye hornswoggler!" she said, getting out her rubber cutlass. The other pirate yelled "Avast!" and pulled out his fake knife and they fought for a minute, until the boy quit and ran to catch up with his friends.

"Run, like the scurvy dog ye be!" Reggie yelled after him.

Anyway, it wasn't really a fair fight because his knife was way too short for her sword.

One old house was completely dark except for a dim light on the porch. We reached the front and heard a terrible scream that sounded real. We all looked at each other.

"Let's not go here," Elmo said. "Anyway, I think they're not doing Halloween."

"I'm not scared. I want my candy!" Reggie said and charged up the walkway, Zander behind her.

The rest of us followed. Spooky sounds came on, like an old door creaking open and slow, heavy steps. We all looked at each other. Suddenly the door flew open and a monster came out roaring and grabbed Reggie around the neck and the back of Zander's vest as he started to run away. We mermaids all screamed. Then the monster pulled off his head mask and it was a guy, and he was laughing.

"How did you like my Halloween trick?" he asked. "It's too scary for most kids this year." Even though he had tricked us, he showered us with candy and even shouted at our mothers to come and get some. "Come on up here! I can't eat all this myself!"

After a while Elmo was walking slower and slower and lagging behind us. He kept complaining about his feet being cold and hurting.

"I told you to wear shoes," Reggie grumbled.

"Whoever heard of a parrot with shoes." Finally Elmo said, "I'm going home," and headed off down the street.

"Oh, Elmo, don't be such a drag," Reggie yelled, but he kept going.

"Let me walk you home," my mother said.

"No. Anyway, I live right there." He pointed at a house down the street.

After he left we went to a few more houses, but we were all getting tired, and anyway we already had lots of candy. Reggie and Zander weren't tired, but Kitty said she had to get home, so we headed back to Reggie's house for the car and my mother drove Bambi and Kitty home.

"Thank you for the ride, Mrs. Barcela," Bambi said. "And thank you for taking us trick-or-treating. It was so much fun!"

"Yes, thank you, Mrs. Barcela!" Kitty said. "See you at school tomorrow, Camile."

"Well, it looks like you're making lots of friends. Is it fun?" my mother said on the way home.

I nodded. Having friends was even more fun than it looked!

CHAPTER 35
NEW FRIENDS

The next morning I told Mermary about our Halloween night.

"I liked seeing your friends in their costumes when you came over," she said.

"I was hoping you would see us."

"Is it usual for people to dress up like mermaids?"

"Sometimes, like for Halloween, or a costume party. Oh yeah, some people wear mermaid tails to swim in too, but mainly they do that in swimming pools. I've seen videos on the Internet. It's just girls who do it. Probably because we love mermaids."

"You told me most people don't believe mermaids are real," Mermary said. "Yet humans are so interested in mermaids and write about them and paint them all the time. Why is that?"

"Probably because they *wish* mermaids were real. It must be because they're so beautiful and magical."

"I wish I could be with other mermaids," she said.

I didn't know how to respond, and the early bell rang anyway, so I said good-bye and Mermary and I gave each other wind kisses like we always did.

Kitty was already at her desk when I got there and came over to talk to me.

"Wasn't that fun last night?" she asked. "What did you do with all your candy?"

"My mother let me pick out one piece for my lunch today." Then I remembered to ask, "How about you?"

"I have to hide mine so my older brother doesn't eat it all."

Bambi showed up, but we only had time to say hi before the bell rang and we had to go to our seats.

"Let's talk at lunch!" she said to us, but I didn't know if I was included.

At lunch Kitty and Bambi called me over to sit with them again. We talked about trick-or-treating. They also asked me questions about Zander and Elmo, if they were my friends. I told them about knowing Reggie and them from summer school.

"Do you like one of them? You know, as a boyfriend maybe?"

Except for the night before, I didn't really know them and I wasn't sure what to say. "I liked Elmo's costume. I liked how he made it himself . . . how about you?"

They both giggled.

"They're all right," Kitty said.

"I thought they were nice," Bambi said.

Making conversation was starting to get easier, especially when Kitty and Bambi asked questions. The trick my father told me about asking people the same question back really worked, plus it helped that Kitty and Bambi did most of the talking. Once in a while one of them asked me a question about mermaids. That was an easy subject. They seemed to think I was an expert or something. Otherwise I spent most of the time just listening to them.

That night when he called, I told my father about Kitty and Bambi.

"They might become my friends," I said. "But I'm afraid they might think I'm boring."

"Why?"

"I hardly talk at all. It's hard to think of things to say."

"You know what I do? After I say something, I ask people 'what do you think?' That gets other people talking. I find many non-talkers turn out to be deep thinkers. Maybe because people who don't talk much, spend their time thinking. I think you're one of those kinds, Camile."

I was surprised. I never knew not talking could have a good side.

CHAPTER 36
REGGIE'S HOUSE

Saturday, a couple of weeks later, I was reading a book on evolution, trying to find more information about mermaids. The phone rang, and it was Reggie.

"Elmo and Zander are coming over later and we're going to watch *Pirates of the Caribbean*. Want to come over? Mom's going to order pizza."

"*Pirates of the Caribbean*? I've—" I was about to say I'd already seen it, but my mother turned around from the computer and waved her hand in front of her mouth.

"Hold on," I said to Reggie. "What?"

"Camile, you liked that movie. Do you mind seeing it again?" I shook my head. "Then accept the invitation."

I told Reggie I could come over.

"Great!" she said. "Come over early, say about three, so we can hang out before the guys get here."

When I got there, she was wearing a T-shirt with a skull on the front, a curved knife in his teeth, and "Dead Men Tell No Tales" in a banner. She showed me the DVD we were going to watch.

"This one is *On Stranger Tides*. I got it because it has mermaids. Have you seen it?"

I shook my head. I didn't even know they had made more chapters of that movie.

"We watch lots of pirate movies. Sometimes they have women pirates. Those are my favorites. Come on, let's go up to my room."

We climbed the stairs to the second floor, where she opened a door off the hallway, then I followed her up a second, smaller staircase to the attic. Her room was in one end of the attic. It had slanted ceilings and a window in a little cut-out room at one end. Reggie went over to an old trunk with a humped top and worn leather belts around it. It looked like a pirate's trunk. Inside was a jumble of clothes.

"We always wear something pirate-like when we're going to watch a pirate movie," Reggie said. "I have something you might like."

While she searched the trunk, I looked around at her room. It was completely different from mine. Bookcases were built into the wall with books and stacks of comics, toys and objects like a piggy bank and a little guitar stored there. She also had a desk with a computer, and next to it a bulletin board crammed with papers and postcards and pictures from magazines. On the slanted part of the ceiling were posters, a map, and a Jolly Roger flag. There were bunk beds with dark blue spreads that had stars and moons and astrological symbols. Reggie pulled a grey hoodie out of the trunk and handed it to me.

"Here, try it on," she said.

It had a pink skull and cross bones on it, and the skull had a bow on her head. Underneath was written, "Pirate Girls Rule."

"My grandmother gave it to me."

I put the hoodie on over my sweater.

"Hey, it fits!" Reggie said. "You can have it. It's too girly for me."

"Thank you," I said. "I like your room."

"Doesn't it look like a ship's cabin?" Reggie asked. "There's a room downstairs I could have, but I wanted this one. It's a gable, that's why it has a slanted ceiling. That's called a dormer." She pointed at the little cutout room.

"You have your own computer?" I asked.

"It used to be my brother's, but he got a laptop when he went away to college, so I got his old PC. How about you?"

"I use my mother's."

"How do you do your homework?"

"I use her computer in the evenings, after dinner."

"Can you surf the net?"

"No. I'm only supposed to do that with supervision."

"Your mom sounds strict."

"She does?" I had never thought of my mother as strict.

"My brother set some filters for my protection, but other than that, I can look at anything." She went to the window. "Come here, look." The window looked out on the street.

"We can see Elmo's house from here," she said, pointing. "That's his roof right there, the red one. You can see his back door."

Trees and houses were in the way so we couldn't see the whole house, but we had a clear view of the back door, just like she said.

"Want to see something really cool?" She ran out of the room and I followed her to the other end of the attic. There was a door, and next to it, a shelf with binoculars and a telescope. She took the telescope and handed me the binoculars, then opened the door. There were some steps, then a trap door Reggie pushed open and propped with a stick. I followed her out to the roof.

On one side, the roof slanted up, and on the other we could look down on the tops of houses and trees. At the edge of the roof was a narrow walkway, surrounded by a little iron fence.

Reggie headed down the walkway, and I followed, slower because it was scary.

"This house is over a hundred years old," Reggie told me. "This is called a widow's walk. They used to make these so women could come up and see if their husband's ship was coming back from sea."

It was exciting to be up so high. Reggie stopped and pointed to the top of the roof. "Isn't our weather vane cool?" It was of a witch riding a broom toward a crescent moon, and it was a pretty, sort of turquoise color, which I knew was from being stained by the weather.

On the other side of the house we could see far out over the ocean. Reggie knelt down, so I did too, and we looked at the ocean through our instruments.

"Look, there's a tanker," she said. I looked through the binoculars in the direction she was pointing. The ship looked ghostly grey against the sky.

"I wanted to be a pirate when I was a kid. I used to sit out here with my flag and a telescope and pretend I was in the crow's nest of a ship." We watched the ocean for a while. "I've seen whales breaching, and sometimes I see dolphins and seals. Once I saw something that didn't look like dolphins or seals."

"What were they?"

"I thought they might be a school of mermaids," Reggie said.

"Really?"

"Yes. They were breaching, and they looked different in the front from the back."

"How?"

"Well, their skin was different, and I thought I could see heads. Human-like heads."

I thought about this. I knew there had to be mermaids in the area, but if they were so careful about not being seen by humans, would they risk breaching where people could see them from land? They had to know about instruments that helped people see long distances.

I looked at the ocean again but mostly all I could see was water. After a while we heard a yell. It was Elmo, wearing a black shirt with a crooked skull and crossbones on it.

"Ahoy, matey!" Reggie called. "Come in! We'll be right down."

We went back down the little staircase and Reggie closed the trap door. Reggie grabbed her three-pointed hat from a nail in her room.

"Yay!" she said. "Let's go watch the movie!"

CHAPTER 37
A PARTY OF PIRATES

We went downstairs, and I saw that Elmo had probably painted the skull and crossbones on his shirt. Not only was it crooked, but the paint was uneven, going every which way. Yet somehow it looked like something a real pirate would make. Zander showed up a few minutes later. He wore a dark red T-shirt that had a skull with wings and "Flying Pirates" on it, with a picture of a plane on the back.

"You're a different character every time we see you," he said to me. "What's it going to be next time, a whale?" He laughed at his own joke. I didn't know what to say, so I didn't say anything.

"Let's get our drinks, then we can start the movie," Reggie said.

We went into the kitchen and Reggie got out four pint-sized glasses with pictures on them and gave each of us a different one. I got one with palm trees on it. Then she got ice trays out of the freezer.

"There's ginger ale, Coke, and apple juice," she told us. "Fix your drink however you want it."

"Hey, you kids, don't make a big mess!" Reggie's mom called from another room.

"We won't," Reggie called back. "Just a little mess," she said to us and we all laughed.

We put ice in our glasses and poured our drinks. Reggie and I had ginger ale, and Zander had Coke. Elmo said he couldn't make up his mind so he put ginger ale *and* Coke *and* apple juice in his glass, then tasted it.

"It's good," he said. "Anyone wanna try it?"

Nobody did.

Reggie put two bags of popcorn into the microwave, then we carried our drinks to the den. The den had a fireplace with a heater in it and tall windows with drapes that Reggie and Zander pulled closed. Sections of a couch were against one wall with lots of pillows, an old coffee table, and a thick rug on the floor. Zander put his drink and his feet on the coffee table. Elmo sat on the floor. I sat on another part of the sectional. Between two of the couch sections was a projector sitting on top of a DVD player, but there wasn't a TV screen. Reggie put the DVD in the player and turned it on. Trailers started showing on the big white wall opposite us. I was amazed, it was just like a movie screen.

"Isn't this cool?" Reggie asked me. "My brother came up with this idea and set it up."

We watched the trailers while Reggie went back to the kitchen to get the popcorn. She came back with two bowls and gave one to the boys and sat next to me with the other one. We watched the previews and talked about which ones we wanted to see and ate popcorn. Actually, everyone else talked, and I just listened. Finally the movie started.

In the first part, Jack Sparrow, the main pirate character, was trying to escape from the law and got in a sword fight with a pirate who had been using his name. They were crashing around in a storeroom and knocking things over.

All of a sudden, Reggie pointed at one of them. "That's a lady pirate!"

"How do you know?" Zander asked doubtfully.

"Look at her. She's a lot smaller than Jack, plus, she moves like a woman."

We finally got a look at the pirate, and he looked just like Jack Sparrow and I thought Reggie was wrong, that Jack had a twin brother he didn't know about. They kept fighting, then all of a sudden Jack kissed the other pirate, and it *was* a woman. Reggie was right.

In this episode, the English, the Spanish, and the pirates were all trying to get to the Fountain of Youth in the New World. They needed to make a potion that had a mermaid's tear, so they went out on a row boat at night, and beautiful mermaids surfaced around them, singing. Then they turned out to have fangs and were trying to get the sailors. They hissed and shrieked and leapt out of the water.

"Killer mermaids!" Zander said. "Cool!"

The pirates caught a mermaid and carried her with them in a box. In the end, everyone got to the Fountain at the same time, and while everyone was fighting, the mermaid escaped.

When it was over, Reggie turned off the system. "Okay, now let's talk about the movie!"

CHAPTER 38
AN ARGUMENT ABOUT MERMAIDS

"What was everyone's favorite scene?" Reggie asked.

"I liked Blackbeard's magic sword and magic ship," Elmo said.

"My favorite scene was when Blackbeard turned into a skeleton," Zander said. "What was yours?"

"The sword fight scene," Reggie said.

"The sword fight scenes are always your favorite," Zander said.

"So?" Reggie said.

"So it's boring."

"No it isn't. Just because you can't fight."

"Oh yeah? I'll show you."

Zander bent over and pulled a plastic sword out from under the couch. Reggie reached behind the couch pillows and pulled out her cutlass. They started sword-fighting and shouting and jumping on the furniture.

Elmo looked at me. "We always do this."

"Hey kids, go outside if you're going to rough-house!" Reggie's mother yelled. Finally Reggie and Zander settled down.

"Hey, Camile didn't say what her favorite scene was," Elmo said.

"Let me guess," Zander said. "The mermaids."

I nodded.

"Not me," Elmo said. "They were scary."

"Yeah, though it was pretty cool when that first mermaid is all nice and singing, and then all of a sudden grows fangs and starts hissing," Zander said.

"Do you think they were real?" Reggie asked me.

"No," Zander said before I could answer. "You can't just grow fangs, you either have them or you don't."

"Not the fangs, doofus. The mermaids."

"They *looked* real," Elmo replied. "Their tails looked just like goldfish tails."

"Probably because they *were* goldfish tails," Zander said. "They were probably photoshopped."

"They didn't look fake or photoshopped at all," Reggie said. "Usually you can tell."

"They couldn't have been real because there's no such thing as mermaids," Zander said. "What about that one they caught? Her tail faded away and she had legs. It was just special effects."

"That was her, but what about the other ones?" Reggie asked. "We could see their tails from all angles."

"If they're real, how come no one's ever found one?"

"How do you know?" Reggie said. "Maybe someone *has* found one, but no one believed them. Or maybe they didn't tell anyone." She looked at me, and I nodded.

"Or they killed the people who saw them," Elmo said.

"Why would they do that?" Reggie asked.

"Maybe no one ever saw a mermaid because they don't want to be seen. So one day, someone sees one and of course, is going to tell everyone about it. The mermaids would have to kill him."

That would explain why no one had ever seen a mermaid, but I couldn't imagine my sweet and gentle Mermary killing anyone. But what about grown up mermaids and mermen trying to defend themselves? Elmo went back to the kitchen to fix another concoction. Zander and Reggie kept arguing about mermaids.

"Lots of people have seen mermaids," Reggie said. "I know pirates have. It's been documented."

I knew that meant it had been written down in historical books.

"Yeah, and pirates are known to be very honest people," Zander said. Reggie laughed, and then Zander did too.

"This whole world is mostly ocean," Reggie said. "Mermaids could be living someplace that hasn't been explored yet."

"There could be mermaids in outer space," Elmo said, coming back into the room with his drink. We all looked at him. "They were in a comic book I read."

"That's where Elmo gets all his information," Zander said.

"Like you don't read comic books," Reggie said.

"Yeah, but I don't believe everything I read in them, like you guys."

"How do you know there aren't mermaids in outer space?" Reggie said.

"Oh no, here we go again," Zander said. "What do they do, fly around with fishbowls on their heads?"

Reggie's mother stuck her head in. "You kids about ready for pizza?" she asked.

Everyone said yes.

She looked at me. "We usually get one Canadian bacon and pineapple, and another with sausage and mushroom. Do you like either of those?"

I nodded. I liked any kind of pizza. I hardly ever got any because my mother said it was junk food, but I knew it would be rude to say that. Reggie's mother went to call in our order and Reggie looked at me.

"What do you think, Cam? You haven't said anything."

"She thinks she *is* a mermaid," Zander said. "Isn't there a kind of insanity where people believe they're a mermaid, ickyphobia or something?"

"Be quiet," Reggie said. "I want to hear what Camile has to say."

They were all looking at me, waiting for me to say something.

"Well," I started, "f-from what I read, mermaid tales come from all around the world. I think—"

"Tails?" Elmo interrupted. "How you do you know they're not fish tails?"

"Tales as in stories, dumbo," Zander said. "You know, like in books?"

"Just ignore them," Reggie said to me. "Go on."

"Lots of countries have stories about mermaids," I said. "Some of them are thousands of years old." I paused to take a breath.

"So? What does that prove?" Zander said.

"Quiet, let her talk," Reggie said. "Camile never says anything because everyone else is too busy blabbing."

"I think—I think it means there were m-mermaids everywhere a long time ago," I said. "Maybe we don't see them anymore because they're almost extinct. They could be living in secret places, like maybe a cave in the ocean, or near a secret island or lagoon someplace. Maybe they stay away from us because we had something to do with driving them nearly to extinction."

It was still hard for me to say a lot at one time, but I was getting better at it. It helped that Reggie wanted to hear what I had to say.

"Maybe humans ate them," Elmo said. "Maybe they taste really good. That would explain why they stay away from people now."

"Do you think the mermaids in the movie were real?" Reggie asked me.

I had been thinking about this, because although they didn't look like Mermary, and they had five fingers, I had a theory that there were probably different races of mermaids, just like humans. That's why mermaids looked different from each other sometimes.

"Yes," I said. "I think Hollywood has some mermaids that act in movies, and they keep it a secret."

"That's absurd," Zander said. "How could a half human live in water all the time? They'd be half wrinkled up all the time, not those smooth chicks we saw in the movie."

"You're absurd," Reggie said. "Chicks are fuzzy baby chickens and can't live in water. Furthermore, mermaid skin would adapt to being in water all the time. Humans are the most adaptable animal on the planet."

"Oh, so now you're saying mermaids are descended from humans?" Zander asked, shaking his head like he thought she was crazy.

"Maybe . . ." I started, and everyone looked at me. "M-maybe they evolved from humans." I was thinking about the book I was reading earlier. Everyone looked at me again.

"Um . . . scientists think we evolved first into fish, right? When the whole world was covered with water. Then um, from fish, to live on the land."

Everyone was waiting for me to say more.

"It's just that . . . um . . . maybe some people lived on both land and sea for a long time, and people split off and became humans, and the other ones evolved so they had fish tails. That means mermaids *are* descended from humans."

"Why would they do that?" Elmo asked. "Go back into the sea?"

"Yeah, wouldn't that be de-evolution?" Zander asked. He changed his voice. "'We are *Devo*.'" He laughed at his own joke again.

Elmo jumped up and started singing and dancing like a robot.

"'We are Devo. D-E-V-O.'" He walked stiff-legged until he banged into the wall and rubbed his forehead, which made us all laugh.

"No. It's still evolution," Reggie said. "Evolution always happens in pursuit of food. Maybe there got to be too much competition on land."

I nodded. We talked about it some more, until Reggie's mother came in with two pizza boxes. The pizzas were huge and steaming, and smelled so good.

Reggie tore paper towels off a roll and gave a couple to each one of us. After everyone had taken a slice, I took one with Canadian bacon and pineapple because I'd never had it before. It tasted wonderful. It was fun to be at my first ever pirate party. Reggie was really fun, and she was smart too. I couldn't wait to tell Mermary all about it on Monday.

CHAPTER 39
A MERMAID'S CAVE

I asked my mother to drop me off at school extra early so I could go to church, but really it was because I had a lot to tell Mermary. I told her all about Reggie, her house, and the movie, and then about the sword fight and our argument about whether mermaids were real or not. Mermary loved hearing about the mermaids in the movie, but she thought the argument was really funny. When she laughed, she rolled and turned somersaults in the water and laughed in a watery, burble-y way that always made me laugh too.

"Mermaids are real, as real as real can be, I'm proof. Humans love mermaids, and yet they don't want to believe in them to the point that they fight about it. Are people always mixed up about things?"

"Sometimes, yes." I stopped giggling. "It's good that most people don't believe in mermaids, or there would be a lot more people out looking for them."

"What's the big deal? If someone looks toward me, I swim away really fast, even faster than fish. I don't even think about it, it's instinctual."

Maybe that's where the stories and art all came from, people seeing a mermaid, and the mermaid disappearing so fast, it made them think they had imagined a half human person with a fish tail. Mermary had something to tell me too.

"I found a little cave on one of the bird islands. The dirt washed out of a little area next to rocks, and the roots of a tree grow down into it. It's moist, and I've been staying there. I keep things from the lake that I find there."

The bird sanctuary had several little islands that had been built very close to the shore so people could bird watch. Nearby was a Regional Park Ranger's building, where the park service had an office. They took care of the birds. Near to the center was the boathouse, where people could rent boats, or launch them if they owned one.

"Mermary, more people go to that area than any other place on the lake."

"I know. But I'm careful. I go to the cave only after it gets dark. Besides, I always see people before they see me."

"You do?"

"Yes. It's almost like I can see behind me. That's how I can disappear so fast."

"Mermary, are you happy in the lake?"

"Yes, I love it here! Thank you so much for giving me such a wonderful, big home."

I was glad that Mermary loved the lake, but I secretly felt a little guilty because, like my mother told me about the baby shark I'd found, Mermary probably really belonged in the ocean. I put her in the lake because I couldn't bear to set her free in the huge ocean. Not only would she be in more danger there, I might never see her again. The warning bell at school rang, so we blew kisses and said good-bye.

CHAPTER 40
PRESENTS

A few weeks after the Pirate Party, Reggie's mother called my mom and invited us to a holiday bazaar at their church. Then Reggie got on the phone and asked me if I could spend the night.

"I have some mermaid videos I want to show you," she asked. "And I got a mermaid DVD for us."

My mother said I could spend the night and helped me pack my overnight bag. I was so excited. Lots of girls in my class had sleep-overs, and it always sounded like so much fun. I put a school book into my bag, but my mom took it out.

"Overnights are supposed to be fun, Camile. You're not supposed to do homework. Save that for when you go to a study group."

We all went in Reggie's mother's car. The bazaar was being held in the auditorium, which had been decorated with holly, red poinsettias, and garlands of pine. There were tables of baked goods and crafts. There was also a section for a flea market, which was where Reggie and I headed.

"Camile, don't leave the building without telling me," my mother said. Reggie's mother winked.

Since it was going to be Christmas soon, I mostly looked for presents. I found a book on Stephen Hawking for my dad and a vase shaped like a dolphin for my mother. Reggie looked at everything, even things she didn't want, and talked to the vendors about what they were selling. She wasn't shy at all, and didn't have a problem talking to anyone. At one stall, a woman was selling diving equipment.

"Are you a diver?" Reggie asked.

"No, my daughter was," the lady replied. "She moved to the Midwest for a job and asked me to sell her gear."

I found a small stainless steel knife that I thought was perfect for Mermary, now that she was getting bigger. It came in a rubber sheath that had two straps. The lady told me it was supposed to be strapped to a person's thigh. Mermary would only need one strap to wear it, and I could make more holes in it so she could wear it around her waist. The lady told me it was eight dollars. Now I had a Christmas present for Mermary too. Reggie saw me putting the knife in my bag.

"Hey, can I see?" Reggie asked. "A diver's knife. What's it for?"

"Oh—I'm going to give it to my mother for Christmas," I lied.

"You already got her a present. Does she dive?"

"Sometimes," I said. Actually, my mother didn't dive anymore. I hoped Reggie wouldn't find out. "But she can use it for other things in her work. It's stainless steel. It won't rust."

I didn't want to answer more questions, so I pointed across the hall at a man who had piles of comic books.

"Look, comics!"

Reggie looked over. "Sure are! Let's go see what he has."

It's a good thing Reggie was easily distracted. Her knowing about the diving knife made me feel strange because it seemed like a major clue to my big secret.

After we visited all the stalls, Reggie told our moms we were going upstairs to the school so she could show me her classroom. I was surprised that the room and walls and even the windows were messy. Desks were every which way, and there were all kinds of things on the walls, art, maps, quotes by famous people, numbered instructions on how to write an essay, and a great big calendar that had school events and days marked off, but also birthdays written in.

"Look at this!" Reggie pointed to the bottom part of the wall along the back of the room. It was a picture of a dark-skinned mermaid. It was mosaic, but made with paper instead of ceramic or glass.

"It's really nice," I said. "Did your class make it?"

"Yes, but it was my idea to do a mermaid. My teacher got a long piece of paper and drew the shape of the mermaid on it. Then we cut pieces of color out of magazines and glued them on to the different parts of her."

"Your classroom is so different from the ones at my school," I said. "It looks a lot more fun."

After the bazaar we dropped my mom off and went back to Reggie's house. For dinner, Reggie's mom took us out for hamburgers, fries, and shakes, more food that I rarely got to eat. I had a strawberry shake but couldn't finish it, so Reggie finished it for me, even though she had one already. Reggie talked with her mouth open while she ate, which I was taught not to do.

"Wait 'til you see the videos, Cam! People have been catching mermaids on camera and posting them!"

Since I had become friends with Reggie, she had gotten interested in mermaids too, and talked about seeing one "in real life." When we got back to her house, we went up to her room and Reggie signed on and went to YouTube. The first video had been taken by a man. He was above the water, like maybe he was on a hill or in a helicopter. He was over a rock that was close to the shore. It looked like a fish body was lying on the rock, then it moved and I could hear the guy saying, "What's that?" A head looks up from the rock, and it looked like a mermaid with a roundish tail. She immediately scurried to the edge of the rock and jumped off.

The other video showed what looked like the top half of a person underwater. The bottom half of her was dark, and you couldn't tell what it looked like. The mermaid, if that's what it was, disappeared and the person with the camera kept scanning the water, but we didn't see her again.

"Isn't that weird?" Reggie asked. "She never comes up for air. That means she *had* to be a mermaid. Now watch this one . . ."

She brought up another video. In that one, a mermaid was on the shore of an island, lolling around on a beach like a film star. It was several minutes long, and I thought a real mermaid would probably have seen the boat and disappeared into the ocean, like the other two.

"The only thing is, the two mermaids look different from each other," Reggie said. "If you just see one, you would think it was real. But when you compare the two we could see, the mermaids are completely different from each other. If they're real, why are they so different?"

"Well, I have a theory that there are different races of mermaids, like there are different kinds of cats, sharks, or birds, some very different from each other. For example . . . manatees and dugongs, which are related . . . or sharks and whale sharks." I went to Google images and showed her examples of each one.

"You're right," Reggie said. "I hadn't thought about that. So people have probably always caught glimpses of mermaids, but now they're starting to catch them on video."

After we watched them a few times more, I asked Reggie if Zander and Elmo were coming over to watch the mermaid film with us.

"No, because it wouldn't be as much fun. Zander doesn't believe in mermaids and Elmo's afraid of mermaids, which is ridiculous. Anyway, I just want you and me to see it so we can talk about it."

"Really?"

"Yes, you know a lot about mermaids, and you know scientific stuff, so it's fun to talk to you. Come on, let's go get sodas and popcorn, then we can start the movie."

All I could think about as I fixed the drinks was how nice it was that someone like Reggie liked to talk to me, especially because I thought *she* was smart and interesting.

The movie was *Splash*, which of course I had already seen, but I didn't tell Reggie. Anyway, I loved seeing the mermaid in the movie, although I got upset all over again when they captured her. I tried to hide my tears, but Reggie noticed. She paused the movie and gave me a napkin.

"We can turn it off," she said. "I can watch the rest another time."

I shook my head, and we watched the rest of the movie, which of course, had a happy ending.

"They won't really do that when someone finally finds a mermaid, I don't think," Reggie said when it was over. "People have learned to respect whales and dolphins and other animals from Greenpeace, and lots of other organizations."

I nodded, but I knew a mermaid would be in a completely different category from endangered species. People didn't treat other people so well all the time, and mermaids were half-human, or at least looked that way. I didn't know what they would do once they got their hands on a mermaid. And I didn't want to find out, either.

CHAPTER 41
A DOCUMENTARY ON MERMAIDS

The title of the documentary was *Mermaids: Fact or Myth?* It started out with the commentator asking different marine scientists if they believed in mermaids. Most of them said no. A couple made jokes about it. One man got angry and said, "What's this about?" Then, the very last person who was a woman, said, "Science doesn't know everything. I'm keeping an open mind."

Next we saw the same woman getting ready to dive from a boat. The narrator said that the woman was a marine paleontologist and explained that was someone who studied the ocean floor for fossils.

"I've seen some strange things in my work at the bottom of the sea; many creatures that died out millions of years ago. They're preserved in the hardened layer of sand on the ocean floor. Some of them are so strange, giant insects with plated armor and what looks like feathers; a sand-crawler that used protruding rib bones to propel itself across the sand, claws that look mechanical. Compared to them, mermaids don't seem strange at all."

Next they showed several fossils of marine animals. Each one was followed with a cartoon of what it probably looked like when it lived, and how it moved and lived in the ocean.

"Cool animation," Reggie said.

Then the narrator said, "What you are about to see has never been seen by the general public. The scientist who found it has agreed to speak to us only under cover of anonymity."

The camera showed a man sitting in a dark room. All you could see was a bald head because his face and the rest of him had been darkened out.

"I'm a marine archaeologist," he said. "We help to develop a picture of earth's history. Two years ago, I was working with a team studying a particular ocean bed off of the coast of Florida when I came across something I'd never seen before."

They showed a man in scuba gear taking samples from the bottom of the ocean. It looked like he was cutting something from stone. Next the camera showed an image of what looked like a flattened squiggle of a long fish. Then I realized it had a head, I could see what looked like a profile. It also had two long fins where the arms might be. The flippers had five long bones, just like a hand.

"A mermaid!" Reggie shouted.

"A prototype mermaid, I think," I said.

"What's that?"

"An early mermaid from which today's mermaids developed."

The scientist was saying it was the most amazing thing he'd ever seen. "Dozens of scientists have come to study it. Everyone's divided on what it might be. Many say it wasn't a mermaid, it only looked like one, and it had yet to be proved that it was a mermaid.

"I've probably studied and tested this fossil a hundred times," the scientist said. "But what's most amazing, is that its DNA connects this creature to Homo sapiens."

Next there was a scene of a beach, and four people getting their gear out of a Jeep. The same guy spoke in voice-over: "A couple weeks after I found that fossil, myself and several other scientists were preparing to go back to work at the same part of the ocean where we found it." A subtitle came up and said it was a reenactment by actors of something that actually happened.

The scientists stood at the top of a bluff and looked down. Down below were a lot of men standing around on the beach, wearing a strange kind of coverall. A large part of the beach had yellow tape around it. When the scientists began climbing down the bluff with their gear, they were stopped and turned back by uniformed guards with rifles. The camera went back to the bald man in the dark room.

"We had been studying that section of the ocean for more than a year and never had a problem. These people told us they were from some obscure branch of the U.S. government I'd never heard of."

Next it showed the men in coveralls coming up from the beach with a stretcher. It looked like a body was on it, which was completely covered with what looked like a dark plastic sheet.

"After that they built a fence along the coast and posted 'no trespassing' signs." The camera filmed the actual beach, and you could see a high fence had been built, and there was even a man patrolling it, waving the camera away. The camera focused on one of the signs. It said,

NO TRESPASSING
Restricted area reserved
for government research.

"When I found that fossil, I wondered if mermaids or a mermaid-like creature once lived in that part of the ocean," the anonymous scientist said. "When we were kicked off the beach, I figured they found an actual mermaid. The only thing I don't understand is why they would keep it a secret from the rest of the world."

The documentary ended with more interviews of marine scientists debating whether mermaids could be real. Some had really interesting theories.

"Wow, that was amazing!" Reggie said when it was over. "What did you think?"

"I liked it," I said. "Wasn't the fossil interesting?"

"Yes, it looked like a mermaid. It even had a face!"

I didn't say so, but the documentary made me uneasy. I wondered if I could get in trouble for keeping the mermaid a secret from the world. It was a good thing I had never told anyone about her.

CHAPTER 42
A TALK ABOUT MERMAIDS

The day to start giving our presentations arrived. I had done a lot of work on mine. I'd practiced giving it to my parents and Mermary, but I still dreaded having to do it in front of the whole class.

"Don't worry," Mermary said that morning. "Remember, you're an expert on the subject."

"No, I'm not!" I said.

"Yes, you are," Mermary said. "Not only have you been reading about mermaids for months and months, you've actually lived with one. Compared to everyone else, that makes you an expert. That might help you have confidence to speak."

I thought about that as I headed over to school. She was right. Even if I wasn't a true sirenologist, which is an expert on mermaids, and even if I couldn't tell anyone what I *really* knew about mermaids, I *had* read a lot about them.

Sister didn't mention the presentations all morning, through religion, English, or math, or even lunch. No one reminded her either, I think because we were hoping she had forgotten. But immediately after we got back from lunch, she announced we would begin the presentations.

"Students, have the outline you prepared with you. You can refer to this from time to time, but not read from it. And remember to stand straight, speak loudly and clearly, and look at your audience."

Then, taking her gradebook and a timer, she marched to the back of the classroom where she often stood when we were reciting. She called on the first person, a boy named Gregory Abeba, which meant she was going alphabetically. I was fourth on the list. Actually, I noticed that Catherine Ardsdale was absent, so that made me third! I started getting nervous. Barry Baker went next and said something about his grandmother teaching him to knit until the timer went off. It was my turn. Sister had to call on me twice before I could make myself stand up.

"Camile, I know that you're well prepared. You can do this."

I tried to calm down, told myself I was a secret expert. At the back of the class Sister put her finger under her chin to remind me to lift my head. She always coached us with hand signs, like putting her hand behind her ear to let us know we should talk louder, or tapping the top of her head to tell us to stand straight, or her hands to her shoulders to remind us to put our shoulders back. I opened my mouth, but nothing came out. I closed it again.

"Tell us the title of your presentation," Sister prompted.

"Uh . . . M-mermaids. Um, I mean . . ."

Darn! I was already saying "uh" and "um," which Sister was always telling us not to do. I held up my outline and looked at it. I was shaking so badly the paper was rattling. I took another deep breath and cleared my throat. Sister smiled and nodded encouragingly.

"The Mystery of Mermaids," I read.

I saw Bambi and Kitty turn to each other with excited looks. I hadn't told them what my topic was.

Sister nodded. "Okay, go ahead, Camile."

I remembered something she had told us: if you're having trouble, chose two or three people to look at when you're talking. So I looked first at Bambi and pretended I was just talking to her.

"Mermaids . . . um, I mean . . ." I glanced out at the lake and took a big breath. "The b-biggest mystery about mermaids is if they're real or not. But people have always believed in mermaids. 'Lore' means the folklore and beliefs about a subject. Cultures from all around the world have lore about mermaids. The most ancient story about a mermaid is a myth that's thousands of years old, and it's from a country called Assyria. It's about a goddess who turns herself into a mermaid. Another story is from Greece, and it's one of the stories from the Odyssey. That one has killer mermaids in it," I added, remembering what Zander had called them.

Some of my classmates laughed, which surprised me so much, I forgot where I was. Sister pointed at my outline. I looked at it and got back on track. I wasn't shaking as much anymore.

"Most of the stories we have are hundreds of years old. The Disney movie *The Little Mermaid* is from a story by Hans Christian Andersen, and that story is over a hundred and fifty years old. But people still write stories about mermaids. I think it's because mermaids are mysterious, and people tell stories to try to understand them better."

I stopped to breathe and glanced at the classroom. Everyone looked interested. I was calming down. I glanced at my outline to see where I was, then looked at Kitty. Looking at my friends helped me feel more encouraged. I could tell they were interested in what I was saying. I hardly talked when I had lunch with them.

"Part of the mystery of mermaids is superstition. People thought mermaids were magic and could grant wishes and tell the future. But sailors believed mermaids were bad luck because they made storms and caused ships to sink, or lured them to drown in the ocean, so they could eat them.

"In paintings, mermaids are shown with mirrors, combs, or harps. Those are symbols, and symbols are mysterious. Mirrors symbolize a mermaid's beauty. Sometimes they use them to tell the future. Combs symbolize their long hair, and harps symbolize their singing, because mermaids love music.

"Mermaids are also connected with the moon, probably because the moon controls the ocean tides. So mermaids are symbols of the sea, of good and of evil, and music and magic . . . I also think mermaids are a symbol for secrets, because there's so much secrecy about them."

I was finished with my presentation. I took a big breath of relief. I looked around at everyone staring at me. Then Bambi started clapping, and then everyone else did too. I was surprised because so far, no one else got clapping. Sister was beaming. She nodded and I went to sit down.

"That was totally awesome, Camile!" Kitty said as I passed her.

Some of the kids around her nodded.

I smiled. I was so glad to be finished!

CHAPTER 43
THE MERMAID GIRL

After my presentation, other girls in my class started talking to me. They noticed when I checked books out on mermaids and asked me about them, or they asked me for titles of good mermaid books. A couple of girls asked me to teach them how to draw mermaids. Once in class, when we were talking about mammals that live in the ocean, someone asked if mermaids were mammals.

Wanda, the most popular girl in class looked at me. "Why don't we ask the mermaid girl?"

I couldn't help but smile. I loved that she called me "the mermaid girl." It was like a compliment.

Sister looked at me. "What do you think, Camile?"

"Actually, I-I've thought about it a-a lot," I stammered. "M-mermaids could be mammals because they breathe air and have hair, except mammals don't have scales. So I think mermaids would be in a c-class of their own, one that hasn't been invented yet."

"Very good," Sister said. "Camile has pointed out that mermaids have scales, which mammals don't have, and that mermaids don't fit into any of the phylum that currently exist. And what is a phylum?"

No one answered.

"A phylum is a category that scientists use to separate out organisms from one another," I said. "Mammals and reptiles are examples of a phylum." I knew that because my mother had explained it to me lots of times.

Everyone, even Sister, was staring at me, like they were waiting for me to say more.

"S-so, if a mermaid is ever found, scientists would have to figure out which phylum she belongs to, based on her characteristics, like hair, and whether she's warm or cold-blooded. Stuff like that."

After that, "The Mermaid Girl" became a sort of nickname, and pretty soon, it spread to the whole school. Kids from other grades started talking to me too, asking me questions about mermaids, or telling me about books or movies with mermaids that they saw. A boy named Will told me he thought he saw a mermaid when he went to Hawaii. He showed me a photograph on his phone. At first it just looked like a woman with her head out of the water, then I saw what looked exactly like a fin behind her, sticking up out of the water.

"When she saw me, she ducked and she didn't come back up for air," Will said. "I was on shore, but I watched for about half an hour. I never saw her come up again. People can't stay under water that long!" Then he asked me not to tell anyone because he was afraid people would think he was silly. Of course, that was an easy secret to keep, and I was an expert at keeping secrets.

Little girls from the lower grades asked questions about mermaids, like if mermaids were real, and if I had ever seen one. I told them mermaids were real, and I had seen one near the ocean, which was the truth.

A girl named Nela invited me to my first ever slumber party. "We're going to tell scary stories," she said. "Are there any scary mermaid stories?"

"Actually, lots, because a lot of people are afraid of mermaids. They even call them monsters." I thanked her for inviting me, and said I would tell a couple of mermaid ghost stories. Nela clapped and was excited.

One day at lunch, Kitty brought up the talent show the school had every year before closing for summer. "Anyone can be in it, if they have an act. I think we should sign up."

"But what would we do?" Bambi asked.

"We could learn a mermaid song like 'Under the Sea.' My mom used to be a music teacher and coached singers. I'll ask her if she'll teach us the song. We could wear our Halloween costumes."

"Yes! Let's do it!" Bambi said. "Want to?" she asked me.

I nodded.

"It'll be really fun," Kitty said. "But we have to start learning the song right away. Can you come to my house on the weekends to practice?"

Bambi said yes and I nodded. Even though the thought of singing in front of the whole school sounded scary, I really wanted to hang out with Kitty and Bambi, plus have an excuse to wear my mermaid costume again.

So, without even trying, I had become popular in a way. Not like the most popular girls in class like Wanda or Jeannie or Nela, who had good personalities and could talk to anyone, but a special popularity that came from my knowledge.

There was just one person, an eighth grader, who didn't seem to like me. She would stare at me, and when she did, she didn't have a nice expression on her face. I felt kind of nervous when I saw her watching me, but she never said anything to me.

There was another downside to my popularity. Sometimes my classmates wanted to walk home with me, or they would invite me to do something after school. Because I wanted to make friends, and because I really wanted to do it, I would say yes, but that meant I couldn't visit Mermary as often after school. Mermary didn't mind, but I did.

CHAPTER 44
QUESTIONS

Bambi and Kitty were my best friends at school, we had lunch together and got together on weekends. But Reggie was my best friend out of school. She became as interested in mermaids as me, and it was fun to talk about them with her. I showed her how to draw mermaids, and pretty soon she was drawing them better than me. She had artistic talent and wanted to be a cartoonist when she grew up. She already drew comic strips that were silly, sometimes about us. They were always fun to read.

When Reggie found out what my mother did, she asked a lot of questions, like what they did at the research center, if they had a lot of tanks, how they studied the animals, and if they dissected them. She also asked if they had endangered species at the center.

"I think that's the main reason they're there, so they can study them and do research."

"But if they're endangered, shouldn't they set them free so they can have babies?"

"They do, but only when they're sure the animal can survive on its own again. They only keep animals that are sick or injured so badly they wouldn't be able to find food anymore, and would suffer and die in the wild. Having an endangered animal to study can help the whole species because my mother and other scientists look for ways to help them. They also use them for teaching people about wild animals."

"If you found an endangered animal, would you give it to the center so they could take care of it?"

"Definitely."

"You would?"

I nodded.

"What about that little shark you found, why didn't you take that to the center?"

"My mother said it was a tiger shark, and it wasn't endangered, plus it wasn't injured."

Reggie stared at me. "Cam, do they have a mermaid there?"

"I don't think so. My mother would have told me."

"But what if it's top secret, you know, like in that documentary we saw? It said the government may have found a dead mermaid, and it was top secret. You said that place your mother works is a government research center."

I was pretty sure they didn't have a mermaid there, or my mother wouldn't mind that I was so interested in mermaids. Reggie kept looking at me and waiting.

"Would you like to go there sometime?" I asked. "I'll ask my mother if she'll take us."

"Really? Will we be able to see the whole place?"

I nodded. I asked, and my mother said she could take us the very next weekend.

CHAPTER 45
THE MARINE RESEARCH CENTER

My mother was glad we were taking an interest in marine science. On the way down to the center, she told Reggie about it.

"We do research on marine life at the center. We're also a teaching facility. We get students from the university in Santa Cruz who are taking classes in marine biology, but lots of other schools come on field trips to see the center, or even hold a class."

"Are you a teacher too, Ms. Barcela?" Reggie asked. She was sitting in the front seat.

"I've taught a few classes, but mostly the instructors are from the universities."

"Do you take the students scuba diving?"

"I used to, but not anymore. I only have a part time job right now, and scuba diving takes up a lot of time."

Reggie turned around and gave me a questioning look. I was afraid she was going to ask about the diving knife, but then Reggie changed the subject and started asking about endangered species.

"Right now we have a Guadalupe fur seal that someone shot and we're bringing back to health, and some tidewater gobies we're studying," my mom said. "And a couple of small green sturgeon because they're one of the Species of Concern. That means they're threatened and we need a lot more information about them to find out if they should be on the Endangered Species list. We also have a beautiful little loggerhead sea turtle that someone found tangled in a net. We'll be releasing her next week, which is why it's so great we're going this weekend. There's also a California tiger salamander someone brought in. Those are getting rare."

"What about sea serpents?" Reggie asked. "I saw a picture of one. It took sixteen sailors to hold it. Have you ever had one of those at the center?"

My mom smiled. "You probably mean an oarfish. That's actually a fish, a very long one."

"Oarfish were often mistaken for sea serpents," I said. "When they're sick, they swim near the top of the water sometimes."

"That's true," my mother said. "But they're found in warmer water than we have around here, so we haven't had one at the center."

"What would you do if someone brought in a mermaid?" Reggie asked.

"Well, that would be a huge sensation, and scientists would be coming from all over the world to see it. Not just scientists, but the public too. I'm not sure the center could manage that many people." I could tell my mom was enjoying all the questions Reggie was asking.

"You could if you kept it a secret." Reggie watched my mom while she asked these questions.

"True, but that would be such an important discovery, it wouldn't be ethical to keep it a secret."

"What if you just kept it a secret for a while, until you were finished studying her? Then you could announce to the world that you had a mermaid."

"We could do that, and it might even be a good idea. That way, we could decide how we would manage the crowds before we told the press."

Reggie gave me a knowing look. I wondered if she was still thinking there was a mermaid at the center. Sometimes it almost seemed as if Reggie knew something about the mermaid, but I didn't see how that was possible. I had never told anyone.

We reached the research center and pulled into the staff parking lot. The center was open to the public on the weekend. All the cars in the public parking area meant a lot of people were already there, even though it was early.

First we went into the visitors' center and looked at all the displays and posters and charts of ecosystems. There were a couple of big aquariums with live fish and kelp we could look into. Other smaller tanks had been made to look like a tide pool with anemones growing off the rocks, hermit crabs, limpets, starfish, and even a sea urchin. Lots of little crabs were eating part of a fish that had been put in there. A machine simulated waves so water washed over everything every few minutes.

After that my mother took us into the back and showed us where she worked. The public wasn't allowed back there. We got to see tanks of all sizes with different animals in them. All the tanks had filtration systems that cleaned the tank and pumps, kind of like my aquarium. She showed us which ones were the endangered species, including the loggerhead turtle, which was amazing. I noticed Reggie looking at a door that said,

Restricted Area—No Admittance.
Staff Only.

My mother led us over to a swimming pool-colored tank with an orange-ish octopus.

"This is a Pacific coast octopus," she said. "He's not endangered. He's here for research purposes. We won't keep him too long, because he'll grow too big for our tanks. He's also one very smart cookie. He somehow knows there's fish in the other tanks, and if we didn't put a locked lid on his tank, he'd sneak out and eat them."

"You mean he can get out of his tank and go over to the other tanks without water?" Reggie asked.

"Not only that, but after he eats them, he gets back into his own tank, thinking we won't know. When we first got him we thought he was too small to be a threat to the other fish in here. We found out the hard way when fish started disappearing."

My mother let us touch it. It felt like it looked—slimy. The octopus seemed like it was checking us out at first, then it pulled back his arms. Reggie seemed mesmerized by the octopus.

A man and woman came to talk to my mother about the wounded seal. They were concerned because the seal looked "listless."

"Mom, can we see the seal?" I asked.

"Maybe. Let me go back and check on her. You and Reggie stay here and look at the animals. Remember, don't touch them or the tubes that feed into the tanks."

As soon as we were left alone, Reggie pointed at the door to the restricted room. "What's in there?"

"I don't know."

"You've never been in there?"

I shook my head.

"Let's go see!"

"What if we're caught?"

"What are they going to do, send us to juvie?" She ran over and tried the door. It was unlocked. "Come on! Your mother said they could be secretly studying mermaids here."

Of course, that's not exactly what she said, but I followed. Actually, I had wondered what was back there too. The room was like a big warehouse, and at the end was a wide door like a giant garage door. There was also a channel where a boat could come in from the ocean.

"This must be where they first bring animals and samples in," I said.

There were a lot of tanks like in the last room, but some were bigger. Reggie ran around and looked into all of them. Not all of them had fish in them, and the ones that were in there didn't look healthy. Out of one popped a seal, right into Reggie's face. We both jumped back, and then we laughed.

"He probably thought you were going to give him a fish," I said. "You know, like at the zoo?"

Reggie reached out to pet him but he quickly slipped back down in to the water.

"It's better not to touch them," I said. "We could give him germs, or he might give them to us."

"Is this the Guadalupe fur seal your mom was talking about?"

"No, I think it's a young elephant seal. See his nose? He's a male. And look—he's got a cut all around his middle that's healing. That's probably from a fishing line."

"Hey, look at that!" Reggie said, pointing across the room. It was a big tank with Plexiglas sides, half full of water, although there wasn't anything in it. She ran over to it. I kept checking the restricted door to see if anyone was coming.

"Cam, this tank is just like the one they kept the mermaid in that movie, *Splash*. And look, there's even big scales on the bottom!"

It did look like there were scales at the bottom of the tank. Reggie looked at me.

"They could have had a mermaid in here!"

"But where would she be now?"

"I don't know. Maybe they studied her for a while, and then she told them mermaids are endangered, and asked them to let her go, and they did. Or maybe . . . wow, maybe she died? Your mother said they usually get injured or sick animals. That might be how they got a mermaid, and they've kept it secret."

"That's good then," I said. "Don't you think?"

"Yeah," Reggie admitted. "But it sure would have been cool to see a live mermaid."

I wondered what my mother would say if she caught us in here. "Reggie, we probably should get back. We might get in trouble for being in here."

She took another long look around and finally said, "Okay."

We slipped back out the door, and we had just closed the door when the opposite door opened and my mother came back.

"Come on, girls. I can let you have a quick look at the seal." She didn't even seem to notice we were standing right in front of the restricted door. Reggie and I looked at each other and tried not to giggle.

Later, when we were by ourselves in my room, Reggie said, "I thought you told me your mother does scuba diving."

For a minute I didn't know what to say. "Well, once in a while she does, like when we went to Mexico for a vacation."

"I thought you said she did it for work?"

"She can use the knife in her work here, or *if* she does some diving," I said.

After that, Reggie dropped it. I had learned in school that you should never lie, because one lie leads to another. We'd never gone to Mexico for vacation. I just hoped Reggie wouldn't ask my mother about scuba diving in Mexico—or about the knife I had supposedly given her.

CHAPTER 46
A SIGHTING

One day in March, right after the three o'clock bell rang, someone tapped my shoulder. It was Will, the boy who saw a mermaid in Hawaii.

"Camile, did you hear someone saw a mermaid in Lake Meredith?"

"What?" I was shocked.

"Yeah, isn't that cool?"

I didn't think it was cool at all. I was scared.

"Do you think it's true?" Will asked.

"No," I said. "Mermaids live in the ocean." But if Will was reading lots of stories about mermaids, he would know mermaids also live in rivers and lakes and wonder why I was lying. "Actually, mermaids used to live in lakes or rivers, but not anymore. I'm not sure why. Who was it that saw the mermaid?"

"David Toledo, he's in the sixth grade. He was fishing with his mom at the far end of the lake last weekend. You know how the sea fish come in from the estuary? The water is a little shallow in places down there. David said he was just sitting there staring at the water, and then he saw something moving underwater. It was chasing a fish. He swears it was a little mermaid, about that big—" He held his hands apart about a foot, which was Mermary's size. "He said she snatched the fish and zipped away."

All I could do was stare at Will with my mouth open.

"So then David starts yelling, 'A mermaid! A mermaid!' His mother told him to calm down and tell her what he saw. Some of the fishermen said sometimes your mind wanders and you see things when you fish. Another person said maybe what he saw was a mud puppy, which is a giant salamander, but we don't have those here. David says she had long hair and hands, and a long fish tail."

"Wow," was all I could say.

Will said he was going fishing with David that weekend and they were going to look for the mermaid. "I'll let you know if we see anything."

"Thank you," I mumbled.

I wanted to head right over to the lake, but then a new girl named Emily, who was African-American, came over and showed me a book.

"This is *The Water-Babies*, it's about water fairies. They're not exactly mermaids. It's my favorite book. Would you like to borrow it?"

I had already read it, but took the book to be polite. Emily kept hanging around while I got my homework books and papers and stuffed them in my knapsack.

"Want to walk home together?" she asked.

I had to talk to Mermary, but I didn't want to be rude and tell Emily to go away. She didn't have very many friends yet, and I knew what that was like.

"I have to go to the library today. My mother's picking me up there," I said, even though it wasn't true.

"Can I go with you?"

"Sure," I said, though I was feeling really anxious.

At the library I showed her some mermaid books. Then we sat down at a table and started our homework.

"What do you keep looking at?" she asked.

"What?" I realized I kept staring out the back doors of the library, at the lake. "Oh, just the lake. It's so pretty."

"I heard Will saying there might be a mermaid in the lake."

"You did?"

She nodded. "Do you think it's true?"

"No!" I said too loudly, and Emily looked surprised. So I had to force myself to say, "But wouldn't it be neat if there was?"

"I think it might be true. Maybe we can go look for her sometime?" she asked.

"I'd have to get special permission. I'm not supposed to go to the lake." It seemed like Emily was giving me a funny look, then I realized she was thinking about me going there all the time. "I mean . . . to spend a whole day at the lake. We should walk around the whole lake to really get a good look, don't you think?"

She brightened. "What about this weekend?"

"Um, I'm not sure I'll have time, I have to check."

"Maybe you can ask when your mother comes to pick you up."

"My mother—" I almost said my mother wasn't coming and remembered just in time I had lied about that. "My mother will be here late," was all I could say. "But I'll ask her and let you know. Give me your phone number and I'll call you."

Things had been easier when no one ever talked to me. Now to protect Mermary, I was having to lie, and I was doing it more and more. After Emily and I exchanged phone numbers, she said she had to go. She looked happy, and I felt bad because I was misleading her. Of course I had no intention of going to the lake to look for a mermaid. I decided to tell her I couldn't get permission to go to the lake, but ask her to do something else. I watched until Emily was out of sight, then ran over to the landing. I made sure no one was around and called Mermary. After a few minutes, Mermary surfaced.

"Hi, Cammie, I wasn't expecting you—"

"Someone told me today that a boy saw a mermaid in the lake."

Her eyes got big and round. "Really? There's another mermaid here?"

"Mermary, he was talking about you!" I was practically yelling. I tried to calm down. "A boy from my school saw you when he was fishing. It was at the far end of the lake, where the slough is. Last weekend! Were you there?"

"Oh!" She was quiet while she thought about this. "Yes, I was down there last weekend. Certain times of the moon, water comes in from the ocean and brings ocean fish with it. They taste better than the lake fish."

"Mermary, you have to be really careful!"

"But I am careful."

"Please, be extra careful. It would be terrible if people found out about you."

"Why? People would tell stories about me and the lake, like those mermaid tales you've told me."

I started crying. "No. If they knew you were there, they would never leave you alone again. They would probably take you from the lake and lock you up and study you. I've told you all this."

She was swimming nervously, diving and popping up to look at me, then diving again and swimming in small circles. I'd never seen her do that before and realized it was because she'd never seen me crying before. I was upsetting her. I wiped my eyes on the sleeve of my uniform jacket.

"I'm sorry, I'm just scared for you. I want you to be safe."

"I'm sorry, Camile. I promise I'll be even more careful from now on."

I forgot to blow her a kiss when I said good-bye. I called my mother with the phone I could only use for emergencies to tell her I'd be home late (had to make up yet another lie). She said she would come get me at the library.

While I waited, I started thinking about one or two stories I'd read where mermaids lied and were treacherous. So symbolically, you could say they were connected with lies too, which wasn't a nice thing. Only I'd never heard Mermary tell a lie; *I* was the one doing all the fibbing and fudging.

Lying was wrong, but I didn't know how else to protect Mermary. Once in confession, I told the priest about lying so much. He asked what I was lying about, and since priests can never reveal what's said in the confessional, I said, "about the existence of a mermaid. I have a mermaid friend. She lives in the lake now." He chewed me out for lying in the confessional!

"Say a rosary to the Virgin Mary and ask her to help you learn the difference between reality and imagination." Then he slammed the little door between us. I didn't try to confess it again. All I could do was know in my heart, I was lying to protect her.

Anyway, I had a bigger problem. I knew now that even a big lake was too small for a mermaid to live safely around human beings. That was probably the real reason mermaids didn't live in them. I hadn't thought about that before I released her into the lake. Of course, I couldn't think of all the reasons it might be a bad idea ahead of time. That's why sometimes, we have to learn from trial and error.

CHAPTER 47
RUMORS

I didn't hear anything more about people seeing a mermaid in the lake, and I thought maybe I had been worried over nothing. Then one day at school, Bambi and Kitty asked me if I knew anything about it. I thought about saying no, but lying about it might make it worse.

"Will Saunders said his friend thought he saw one. I think it's just a rumor."

"Wouldn't it be wonderful if there really was a mermaid in the lake?" Bambi said. They both looked at me.

"But if there really was a mermaid, wouldn't we know already?" I said.

"Maybe she just recently got there," Bambi said.

"Let's go to the lake after school and see if we can spot her!" Kitty said.

I thought about telling them that my mother had told me not to go to the lake anymore, but they would know that was a lie because I went every morning. So after school I went with them to the lake and stood on the landing where we had taken pictures at Halloween. They put their hands over their eyes to shield them from the afternoon sun and looked out at the water.

"Mermaid!" Kitty called. "Mermaid! Where are you?"

I hoped Mermary wouldn't think that, because I was with Kitty and Bambi, it meant for her to come out. I stood behind them and made the sign for "don't" so Mermary would know she shouldn't come out.

"Look at that guy over there," Bambi said. "He's hiding in the wisteria and taking pictures."

The man had a camera with a big lens on it.

"He might be photographing the mermaid. Let's go ask!" Kitty said.

"I'm not supposed to talk to strangers," I said.

"I'll do the talking," Kitty said.

"You're not supposed to talk to strangers either," Bambi said.

"Only if I'm alone, but it's okay because there are three of us."

I had a feeling she made that up. We went over to the colonnade where the guy stood behind a pillar.

"Hello," Kitty said. "Are you trying to get pictures of the mermaid?"

"No," he said. "I'm a private eye, and I'm working, if you don't mind." He moved further into the leaves that grew around the pillar. He seemed to be staring at two people by the side of the lake. I could tell we were bothering him, but Kitty kept talking to him.

"People have been seeing a mermaid in the lake," she told him.

"Yeah, a mermaid," he said. "Probably the Loch Ness Monster's girlfriend." He pushed his camera through the leaves then glanced around at us. "Hey, I'm sure you're very nice kids, so be nice and go away, okay? If I see a mermaid, I promise I'll take a picture."

Now I knew how rumors got started, and why sometimes they were dangerous. Except this wasn't a rumor.

CHAPTER 48
AN EXCURSION TO THE LAKE

About a month after Will's friend had seen the mermaid, Reggie asked me to go to the wildlife sanctuary at the lake. It was a nice, warm day in April. When she showed up, she had an explorer's hat on and the binoculars.

"Are those for looking at birds?"

"That too, but what I really want to do is look for the mermaid! Have you heard about it?"

I stared at her. She went to school in a completely different part of Luna Beach. How did she know about the mermaid?

"Hello, Reggie!" my mother said, coming downstairs. "Nice to see you."

"Hi, Ms. Barcela. Hey, have you heard that there's a mermaid in Lake Meredith?"

"A mermaid?" My mother stopped on her way into the living room. "Why, no, I haven't."

"Lots of people have seen her. Her upper half looks like a regular girl except she's brownish, sort of like a trout. She has long brown hair and she's really pretty, but when she opens her mouth she has long, sharp teeth. Her fish half looks kind of like salamander skin, mud brown, so it blends in with the lake, and she has a big tail fin shaped like a crescent moon."

For a minute I was afraid my mother believed it, and that was actually worse than disbelieving.

"That's a pretty detailed description, Reggie," my mother said. "Did you see the mermaid yourself?"

"I wish. Jo Jo, a friend of mine told me her mother saw her. She was parked in a car facing the lake, and she saw her jump out of the water after a fish. Jo Jo told me not to tell anyone, but I can tell you because of what you do. Mermaids must be an endangered species since one's never been found before."

"Why aren't you supposed to tell anyone?" my mom asked.

"Her mother doesn't want people to think she's crazy."

My mother smiled at this.

"Wouldn't it be cool if we had our own mermaid, right here in Luna Beach?" Reggie asked me. "Maybe we'll see her today! That would show Thinks-He's-So-Smart Zander."

My mother kissed me goodbye and told us to be careful before we set out. Reggie kept talking about the mermaid.

"I can't believe you haven't heard about it," Reggie said.

"Actually, that rumor is going around my school too, but I didn't believe it," I said. "How do you know about it?"

"Everyone's talking about it."

"What do you mean 'everyone'?"

"The kids at my school. A girl said she and her friend were down by the pier a couple of weeks ago, and they spotted her."

I didn't know what to think. Was it the same rumor going around my school, or had some different kids seen Mermary?

As soon as we got to the lake Reggie swept the water with her binoculars, sometimes handing them to me so I could take a turn. We didn't see Mermary, of course, because as soon as I got there I made the sign for her to disappear. I hoped she really had stopped swimming near boats or hanging out in populated areas around the lake.

Looking at the water wasn't all Reggie did. She also asked everyone we met if they knew about the mermaid. Some old ladies laughed when they heard. She even asked some seven-year-old kids who were fishing.

"A what?" one of them asked.

Reggie described a mermaid to them.

"Oh, like the Little Mermaid," one of them said. "My father said there's no such thing."

"Well, people have been seeing one in this very lake. Tell that to your dad," Reggie said.

I was glum, because every time Reggie talked to someone, more people knew about a mermaid being in the lake and would be on the lookout for her. The only way to get her to stop would be to tell her the truth, but I couldn't do that because I didn't know if she could keep a secret.

We walked by the side of the lake until we reached the bird and wildlife sanctuary. It was taken care of by the Regional Park Services, which had a science center attached to their office. I'd been there before with my mother, and I came on a field trip with my class because it was so close to school. They had stuffed birds and other animals, and an actual beehive with live bees inside a window, so we could see how they worked. There was also a display of animal skulls, and real specimens in jars that Reggie thought was really cool. On the walls were drawings done by children who had come to the center and drawn what they'd seen.

Reggie went to the ranger's office and asked the lady ranger what she knew about the mermaid.

"We've been getting that question a lot lately," she said.

"From who?" I asked.

"All kinds of people. Isn't it exciting? I'm thinking about making a mermaid exhibit. If you kids get any photographs of her, we'd love to have a copy."

"How about drawings?" Reggie asked. "My friend can draw mermaids."

"I'll include mermaid art work," the ranger said, smiling at me. "I like that idea, especially if you catch a look at her. That would make you an eyewitness."

I was miserable. I had thought Mermary would be safe in the lake, but she was being seen, and the rumors were going to be publicized!

We left the ranger's building and crossed over to the fence where people usually stood to look out at the islands. Reggie scanned the little islands with the binoculars, but spent more time searching the water.

"Hey, are you okay Cam?" Reggie asked.

"Yes, why?"

"I don't know. You seem kind of bummed out. Don't you want to find the mermaid?"

I nodded, although I could tell Reggie wasn't convinced. After that I thought I better act like I was interested too. I reminded myself that just because some people claimed to have seen the mermaid, it didn't mean they actually had. Mermary had promised she would be very careful. I decided to take this time to look carefully and notice if I *could* see her, and she just didn't realize she could be seen. She was probably nearby because I was there, and I knew she was curious about Reggie.

At lunchtime we got hotdogs and sodas from a concession stand and found a bench where we could eat and look out at the lake.

"You know what I think?" Reggie said, talking with her mouth full. "That the mermaid must live in a cave on one of those islands. Let's walk around to the other side of the lake and see the back of them with the binoculars."

I didn't say anything, because of course, Mermary *did* live in one of them. But I thought it would be a good idea to find out if her cave could be seen from the other side of the lake.

So after we ate, we double-backed and walked around the lake to the other side. The lake was narrow at this end, so it wasn't that long of a walk, and it took us by Dragon Tree Point where I usually met Mermary. It felt strange because it almost seemed like I was showing Reggie the exact places where I saw a mermaid all the time. We reached the colonnade and I pointed across the street.

"That's Our Lady of the Lake Church, and that building across the courtyard is where I go to school."

"Wow, your church is awesome," Reggie said, stopping to stare. "I know about Catholics and prayers and Jesus and Mary, but I've never been in a Catholic Church. Can you show it to me?"

That was one of the things I liked about Reggie, she was interested in everything. We crossed the street and went inside, and I showed her the little font with holy water and how we used it to bless ourselves. The church inside was high, cool, and dim. No one else was there, only one small candle burned at the side of the altar. We walked down the middle aisle and looked at the stained glass windows, and I told Reggie about the statues of the saints.

"So, who is the Lady of the Lake?"

I pointed at the statue in a niche next to the altar. Our Lady of the Lake was a creamy white statue with her hands held out. I led Reggie over to it.

"The mother of Jesus takes on lots of different forms around the world. Our Lady of the Lake is one on them." I told her what Sister told us about her. "Even though she's white, the original back in Europe was black, so she's still considered a Black Madonna. They're very holy, and grant miracles. Hundreds of years ago there were lots of Black Madonnas, but now the Catholic Church paints some of them white. Because of, you know, racism, but also because they're trying to hide their former roots, which are pagan, not Catholic."

"Wait—pagan? I'm confused. Isn't that the opposite of Catholic?"

I tried to think of how to explain it. "You know how Christians go to other parts of the world and convert pagans? Well, say those people worshipped a goddess, that's what made them pagan. Then the missionaries took down the statues of their goddesses and put statues of Mary in her place so that the people would forget about their old goddess and pray to Mary. But Mary is still connected with their old goddess. That's how Mary's roots are pagan. Does that make sense?"

"Yeah. So go on about the Black Madonna."

"Black Madonnas are very miraculous, and they're always connected with miracles and healing water. Most of them are in Europe, but we have one in Mexico, the Virgin of Guadalupe."

"I know about her," Reggie said. "There's pictures of her all over the Mission District in San Francisco. But she's brown."

I nodded. "My teacher said that any Madonna who isn't white is considered a Black Madonna."

"How about a green one?"

I blinked. "Have you see a green one?"

"I saw a picture of a carving from a castle in Europe. There were leaves all around her, and she was holding the baby Jesus. She was painted green."

I shrugged. "I guess so."

I knelt down on the kneeler in front of Our Lady of the Lake and put fifty cents in the box so I could light a candle, then said a prayer, silently asking the Virgin Mary what I always asked her: to keep Mermary safe. Reggie knelt too, but she kept looking at the statue.

"Cam," she said when I finished praying. "Could The Lady of the Lake secretly be a mermaid?"

"A mermaid?" I had thought bringing Reggie here would take her mind *off* mermaids.

"She looks like a mermaid," Reggie said.

I looked up. Of course I had seen her hundreds of times, and I never thought she looked like a mermaid. Her long dress was very slim and covered her legs and feet.

"Look at the bottom of her skirt," Reggie said.

The bottom of her dress turned out sideways in both directions, and was carved very gracefully in a way that actually looked like they could be waves, or even a half-moon on its back, with curly ends.

"Her dress could be hiding a tail, that's why the bottom of her dress is spread out like that," Reggie said. "Actually, it sort of looks like it could *be* a fin."

She was right, I had never noticed it before. I told Reggie we should leave so we could talk about it. I wasn't sure if it was disrespectful to talk about green Marys, and Mary being a pagan mermaid, in church.

Outside, I told Reggie, "One of the books I read said that a long time ago, there were cultures that worshipped mermaid goddesses. I know Our Lady of the Lake is from an ancient European culture that was on the coast of the Mediterranean Sea, the same area that had a mermaid goddess. So maybe you're right."

"Cool! A Catholic Virgin Mary of mermaids!"

That sounded funny and I laughed. We crossed the street back to the lake. I was glad I had prayed, I was feeling a lot better, a lot less scared than I was earlier. We walked along the side of the lake until the islands were across from us, but even with the binoculars we couldn't see anything that might be a cave. I was glad we had done this, because I felt a lot more secure that it couldn't be seen. After that we went home.

I thought some more about Our Lady of the Lake being a mermaid. If Reggie was right, it really was cool, even magical. More importantly, I was sure Mary of the Lake would keep Mermary hidden and safe, because she was one of her own.

CHAPTER 49
PHOTO EVIDENCE

The rumors at my school didn't stop. They got worse. Then one day when I got to school, a bunch of girls were gathered around Kitty and Bambi. I went over to see what they were looking at.

"Come here, Camile, look!" Kitty said.

She showed me one of the pictures her mother had taken of us on the landing at Halloween. "I was looking at our Halloween pictures this morning and I noticed this. There's four mermaids!"

I looked at the photo but I didn't know what she was talking about. Then Kitty pointed to the water behind us, and I gasped. The late afternoon sun was shining through the water, and there was a shadow that looked exactly like a mermaid shape. It was Mermary.

"The mermaid came to look at us in our mermaid costumes!" Bambi said.

All I could do was stare with my mouth open.

"It's just a shadow though," one girl, Tricia, said doubtfully. "It's not a picture of an actual mermaid, so it could be something else, like maybe a piece of wood floating in the water."

I nodded, glad that someone else had pointed that out.

"Well, I think it's the mermaid," a bossy girl named Allie said.

"Me too," Susan said.

Everyone was excited about it. Jeannie, one of the popular girls, was looking at me.

"Camile, have you ever seen the mermaid?"

I shook my head.

"Some first graders told me you had," Allie said.

"I—I thought I saw a mermaid once, but I'm n-not sure if that's what it was," I stammered. "Anyway, that was near the ocean, not the lake."

"Why do you go to the lake every morning?" Nela asked.

"Yeah, why?" Allie asked crossly.

Everyone was looking at me now. I had known that sooner or later, someone was going to ask me this, and I already had an answer planned. "The lake is really beautiful in the morning. I go there to meditate and pray. Remember how Sister told us we could meditate anywhere?"

"Okay, so why do you go again after school?" Allie asked.

"I don't."

"You used to," Tricia said.

"Because—because I love the lake."

"I think you're seeing the mermaid," Allie said. "Why don't you want to tell us about it?"

"Please tell us!" Kitty begged.

"Yes, do!" Bambi said. "Please?"

I tried to think of what to say. "Well, I . . . I've seen things that could have been a mermaid, but . . . but they were like that picture, not an actual mermaid."

"You've seen something like what's in the picture?" Bambi asked.

I nodded reluctantly. All the girls looked at each other with amazement.

"So there *is* a mermaid!" Jeannie said.

"No, what I said—" I tried to explain, but they were all excited and talking and saying, "Camile has seen the mermaid!" and it was obvious they only heard what they wanted to hear.

"Let's all go to the lake sometime and look for the mermaid!" Jeannie said.

Everyone said yes except me. I had made the rumors even worse!

CHAPTER 50
RENDEZVOUS

Now I only rarely got to go to the lake to see Mermary, so I came up with a plan. Saturdays I usually went to Kitty's house so we could practice our song for the talent show, and Sundays my mother did the grocery shopping for the week and sometimes went to visit her sister. Instead of going with her like I sometimes did, I had her drop me off at the library. She always told me what time she'd pick me up, which usually was in a few hours. Not only was it enough time to get books and study, I could visit Mermary.

That Sunday my mother dropped me off at the library and said she'd be back at one o'clock. "Are you sure you don't want to go with me? Three hours is a long time to study."

"I'm sure. I want to start on our final project, which is on fifty great men and women. That's going to take a long time."

"Well, okay. But at least take a break studying," she said. "Go outside and sit in the sun for or a while, or maybe go across to the park and swing."

"I will."

In the library I set my books up in a corner with paper and a pen set out, and got the book I had ordered from the librarian. Then I went out, crossed over to the lake, and took the path around it until I reached Dragon Tree Point. I called her and she popped up a minute later.

"Hi, Cammie!" she said.

I was so glad to see her. It had been more than a week since the last time. I told her lots of kids at my school were talking about there being a mermaid in the lake and were looking for her. She promised me that she was being more careful and staying away from crowded areas during the day.

"I'm coming out more at night. The other night a band was walking by the lake, playing horns and something with keys and folds—"

"An accordion," I said.

"An accordion. And people were following behind. Since it was nighttime, no one could see me. I swam along with them so I could watch them and listen to the music. I was looking at their instruments

and watching how they play them. They stopped at that landing—"
She pointed across the lake. "Two people were dancing, and I swam
around to the music."

I thought going out after dark was safer, but just in case I told
her, "People have instruments they use to see at night. They're called
infrared glasses. I don't think they're all that common, but just so you
know, people might be able to see you at night too."

Then I told her about practicing for the talent show with my friends,
and the things I'd been doing, and how much fun I was having.

"I saw you walking around the lake with a red-haired girl. Is that
Reggie?"

"Yes, she's my best friend!"

Mermary didn't say anything as she looked at me. She looked strange.

"Mermary, are you sad?"

"No. I was just wondering if I'll ever see other mermaids. It's really
hard to be alone, and I'm so curious about people."

I realized Mermary was lonely. I felt guilty. I knew there had to be
other mermaids living in the ocean, probably not even very far from
Luna Beach. If Mermary was in the ocean, she might not find them,
but if she was in the lake, she definitely wouldn't.

"Mermary, I'm sorry—"

Suddenly she disappeared. That could only mean someone was
coming. I looked around and saw a girl and a fat lady coming across
the grass toward me. The lady had a red face and a yellow dress
on. The girl wore a baseball cap, a shirt with a large "98" on it, and
shorts. I recognized her. She was that eighth-grader who was always
glaring at me.

"Hello, little girl," the lady said. "Are you looking for the mermaid?"

I shook my head. She introduced herself as Mrs. Crisp and the girl
as her daughter, Helen.

"Weren't you just talking to someone?" Helen said. She walked up
to the edge and looked at the water.

"No," I said.

"Yes you were, I heard you."

"I was practicing a poem from school."

She looked at me like she didn't believe it. "Sure you were. Let's
hear it then."

Luckily I remembered the poem from summer school, and I
recited it.

"That's nice, did you write that?" the lady asked. I nodded. I wondered why she was so nice, and her daughter such a crab. "We're on the lookout for the Lady of the Lake."

"Who's the lady of the lake?" I asked, like I couldn't guess. So, other people were noticing the connection Reggie had.

"The mermaid, Miss Act Innocent," the girl said. I wondered why she was so suspicious.

"The Lady of the Lake is the Virgin Mary. We go to her school," I said.

"Very good," she said sarcastically.

"Is that what people are calling the mermaid now?"

"Why are you acting like you don't know anything about it, *Mermaid Girl*?"

I didn't respond. Was she jealous? Even with a scowl she was pretty, and she was really smart because she won awards for best essays and writing projects.

"I think our church is where people got the idea for the mermaid," Mrs. Crisp said. She opened her tote bag, got out some bread, and threw it into the water.

"Here mermaid, mermaid, mermaid!"

They both watched to see if Mermary would go for it, but I knew she knew better. Pretty soon there were a bunch of little fish eating the bread, and some seagulls landed in the water hoping for some bread too.

"Have you seen anything that might be the mermaid?" Mrs. Crisp asked.

I shook my head.

"I bet you have," Helen said. "You just don't want people knowing this is a good spot to see her."

I wondered if she had seen something, from a distance somehow, but I didn't dare ask. They sat down on the edge and kept looking into the water, so I figured they weren't going to leave. I headed back to the library. On the way, Mermary came to swim alongside me, and I smiled at her but didn't try to talk to her because there were people around. I saw two nuns from my school heading my way. One was my teacher, Sister Marie Anthony, and the other was Sister Daniel, from the third grade. I stopped.

"I understand that people are calling our mermaid The Lady of the Lake," Sister Marie told me. I could tell she was proud.

"Right, our mermaid," Sister Daniel said. "A tourist attraction based on a figment of someone's overactive imagination." She rolled her eyes. "Someone came into the church yesterday when I was removing the old flowers, asking if there was a connection. The church is not a tourist trap."

"One never knows the ways of God," Sister Marie said. "Maybe some of them will take an interest in Him while they're there."

"But they're not. It's Our Lady they're interested in," Sister Daniel said, like it was a bad thing.

"Why is that a problem?" Sister Marie asked. "As the Queen of Heaven, Mary deserves adoration too. She's the one who does all the work up there, interceding with God for us. Women always do the work, and men get the credit." She winked at me.

I said good-bye and headed back to the library. It sounded like everyone in Luna Beach knew about the mermaid now. That's what happens in small towns.

CHAPTER 51
CALLING THE MERMAID

The girls in my class planned an outing to go to the lake and look for the mermaid. They gathered outside in the courtyard after school. Almost all the girls in my class were going, eighteen of them.

"Will you take us to look for the mermaid, Camile, like you did before?" Kitty asked.

"Yes, please?" Jeannie said.

"I can't, my mother's coming to pick me up at the library."

"You can come just for a few minutes," Allie said bossily.

"Please?" Bambi begged. "Your mother never gets here right at three o'clock."

I couldn't believe someone had noticed. They were all standing around me, looking hopeful and excited. I said okay because I didn't want anyone to find out my mother wasn't really coming.

We crossed the street and went over to the landing, then stood by the heavy chain railing that prevented people from falling into the water.

"Camile, call the mermaid!" Jeannie said.

"What should I call her?" I said, trying to stall.

"Just call 'mermaid.' She's probably familiar with you, if she let you see her all those times."

"She didn't let me see her," I said, but it was no use because everyone believed it. So I stood at the edge of the landing and called "mermaid," but not very loudly.

Allie, who was standing next to me, poked me with her elbow.

"Say it louder," she said.

So I yelled, "MERMAID!"

Of course, I had warned Mermary something like this might happen, and to just ignore me if I didn't call her by name. To be doubly sure, I made the hand signal for her *not* to come out, but no one noticed because they were all watching the water. I knew I was misleading everyone, and if they found out, they might all start hating me, and that would be really horrible.

"Look over there!" Jeannie said, pointing. About twenty feet away from the landing was a fountain that sprayed water into the air, and

I could see part of a branch was floating under it. Most of it was underwater, but everyone got excited.

"Is it the mermaid?" Everyone crowded over to get a better look. Kitty clapped and some of the girls jumped up and down with excitement.

"No, it's just a broken branch," Allie said disgustedly. "Call her again, Camile."

I cupped my hands around my mouth and yelled, "MERMAID! Please come and talk to us! Hello! Where are you, mermaid?" I felt kind of silly. Everyone scanned the water that was nearest to us, but of course there wasn't anything to see.

Then I noticed motion in the water off beyond the fountain. I could tell Mermary was turning somersaults under water like she did when she thought something was funny. Maybe we all looked funny to her, calling a branch "the mermaid," and me yelling for something I *didn't* want to happen. I could see the shimmery flashes of her fishtail. She was stirring the water up in such a way that the water over her was mounding up and creating a big, silent disturbance. Emily glanced at me and noticed what I was looking at. She gasped.

"Look!"

Everyone looked where she was pointing. After a moment the motion stopped. Everyone was quiet, continuing to stare at the water to see if it would happen again. It didn't, thank goodness.

"That must have been the mermaid!" Kitty breathed, her eyes shining as she looked at me.

Several other girls nodded, everyone looking at each other with their eyes big. They all looked excited. Of course we hadn't seen anything except an unusual movement of water and the bright, underwater flash of Mermary's tail.

"I saw her big tail!" Emily said.

"Me too," Allie said, turning around to smile at me.

"But . . . maybe it was just a big fish," I said weakly.

"Yes, the big fish half of a mermaid!" Nela said.

"I think I actually saw her top half!" Bambi said.

Emily and Allie nodded.

"Now we can say we've seen the mermaid too," Nela said. "And Camile is the one who brought her to us."

"The mermaid came because she knows you're the Mermaid Girl," Wanda said.

Everyone watched the water for several more minutes, but of course Mermary was still now. She probably had gone to her cave so she could laugh out loud and roll to her heart's desire.

Finally I said I had to go. Kitty and Bambi hugged and thanked me, as did several other girls. Everyone left in different directions, and I headed over to the library until they were all gone. I took out my phone and called my mother to leave a message that I went with a bunch of girls to look for the mermaid. I knew she would like hearing that. Then I hurried home.

I had to admit it was nice to be loved like that by the girls in my class, even though I hadn't really done anything. I was kind of mad at Mermary for going through her antics like that. She probably didn't realize the disturbance it created on the surface, or that it might look suspicious, especially to people who were already on the lookout for a mermaid.

Or had she done it on purpose?

CHAPTER 52
DELIBERATION

Alone in my room that night, I got out my mermaid journal and wrote: "Mermary laughs at people where they can see," and "Mermaids engage in risky behavior."

Then I thought about it. Just because Mermary engaged, didn't mean all mermaids did, so I erased "mermaids" and put in "Mermary." In fact, I was willing to bet that most mermaids never engaged in risky behavior around people, because if they did, we would have caught one by now. No doubt mermaids were taught from birth to always stay away from humans. But Mermary hadn't grown up with mermaids, and I couldn't think of all the ways she needed to be warned about us.

She probably didn't know some of the things she did was risky. She had an instinct to hide from people, but she couldn't stop being curious. It was a natural part of who she was. Curiosity was partly why mammals became intelligent, and part of how she was connected to humans and other primates. Unfortunately, sometimes curiosity could get you into trouble. That's why there's that saying, "curiosity killed the cat."

She was also going to make mistakes. Part of how we all learn is through making them. Like, how was Mermary supposed to know that her way of laughing would cause a disturbance on top of the water that would attract people? How would she know that she could be seen in shallow water?

Maybe her trusting *me* was her very first mistake. And maybe she had a basic need that helped her learn to trust me so that we could hang out and be friends and talk because . . . because mermaids were social. They had a need to be with others, just like humans.

I knew Mermary was lonely. I felt bad because I couldn't keep her company the way I had when she lived in the aquarium. Maybe deep down inside she thought if she was found, she would have company again. Maybe she didn't really believe that people would hunt her, and thought they were all like me. Or she didn't realize how bad being confined to a tank would be; she probably thought it would be the same as when she lived in an aquarium at my house. But I was sure, after she had an entire interesting lake to live in, it would be too hard to go back to an aquarium.

Mermary needed to be in the ocean with her own kind, who could keep her company. They would teach her how to stay away from humans, and help her to understand how humans could be dangerous and even treacherous. Also, there would be many interesting things going on in the ocean to keep her busy.

I should have set her free in the ocean when I had the chance, and now it was too late. I couldn't carry her there by myself. She had gotten so big, I knew she would be too heavy to carry all the way to the ocean in a bucket by myself.

This was a terrible problem, and I didn't know what to do about it. The only thing I could think of was to take her to the ocean in a car, but what adult could I trust with the information that I had found a real mermaid? Certainly not my mother. Although I loved her, and thought what she did for work was important, if I told her about Mermary, there was no way she would allow me to set Mermary free.

And once it got out that mermaids were real, what would happen to all the other mermaids? The government would probably give huge grants to help people find them, and the poor mermaids would be caught and kept in zoos for everyone to gawk at. Maybe they would even be put in water shows and forced to perform tricks, like dolphins and seals and killer whales. I knew sea mammals were actually much smarter than what could be shown in a water performance. I wondered if they felt silly doing tricks, but felt they had to in order to be fed and taken care of.

Maybe those shows were really to demonstrate people's dominance over nature. Maybe they even helped people to feel reassured when they watched them. But we were just fooling ourselves; nature was so much more huge than us.

With so many people knowing about Mermary and looking for her, and Mermary being careless or behaving riskily, maybe other people *had* seen her by now. In any case, it was only a matter of time before she was seen again.

I thought and I thought, trying to figure out what to do to keep Mermary safe, and the existence of mermaids a secret. I had to come up with a solution, and it had to be soon.

CHAPTER 53
THE PIRATE'S SHOW

"Can I come over? I have to show you something!" It was Reggie calling.

Since it was a Monday and a school day, I had to get special permission. My mother said it was okay. I wondered what Reggie was so excited about. Reggie arrived on her bike, and was so excited she didn't even want to wait for the cookies my mother was setting out for us.

"Is it okay if we use the computer, Mrs. Barcela?" she asked.

My mother said "fine" from the kitchen. Reggie went to the computer and opened YouTube.

"This is a pirate show I watch once in a while," she told me. "Pirate Andy Kydd! Have you heard about him?"

I shook my head, but his name was very familiar. I tried to remember where I had heard it before. She clicked on the frame of the video she wanted.

"Look at this."

The screen opened, and in a minute, a video started up. A man with a scraggly beard came on. He had crooked teeth and wore a three-cornered hat and one gold earring. A little microphone was attached to the collar of his authentic-looking blue pirate coat. He was standing in front of a lake.

"Ahoy, Ladies and Gentlemen. I be Pirate Andy Kydd," he said. He sounded like a pirate. "Today I'm investigating rumors about a mermaid who is said to be living in this very lake." He pointed at it.

"That's Lake Meredith!" Reggie said.

I caught my breath. *Oh no!*

"Spring last year brought a series of storms that ravaged this quiet seaside hamlet of Luna Beach," Pirate Andy said. The video showed scenes of huge waves and flooding that had been on the news. Pirate Andy narrated: "Many a sea creature was washed ashore, the poor critters."

Next was some footage of people putting stranded fish back into the ocean. Then the camera showed Pirate Andy sitting at a computer.

He wore a red kerchief on his head and a stripped T-shirt. Using a voice-over, he said, "I established a website back in 2008 where people can post mermaid sightings. Over the years, some people had very interesting tales to tell."

The camera showed a close-up of the same mermaid site I had posted to months ago.

"Just after the storms, someone from Luna Beach posted to this site, claiming to have found a mermaid baby washed up in a puddle. This person provided specific information about her, then mysteriously vanished from the site." The camera did a close up of Pirate Andy, looking directly into the camera. "If Sea Bee is watching this, I beg you, please contact me through my website. I would really like to speak wi' ye."

My mother was just now coming into the living room, bringing a plate of cookies, and I was glad she hadn't heard that. She stood behind us to watch. Pirate Andy was at the lake again, walking toward the camera as it moved backward. I could see Dragon Tree Point in the background.

"Now people are saying a mermaid is living in Lake Meredith, which is located in Luna Beach. Several people claim to have seen the mermaid or something fishy, harr harr—if you'll excuse the pun! My question is: just how did that mermaid get here?"

Next, the camera showed children playing with chicks and baby rabbits.

"Many parents get animals as presents for their children," Pirate Andy narrated. "This is good; it teaches little laddies and lassies about nature and responsibility."

I was glad because it seemed like Pirate Andy was changing the subject.

"Sometimes, when the animals grow up, they become too much for the child to take care of," he said. The camera showed grown geese and chickens, and a big fat white rabbit in a crate. Then the camera showed some large turtles sunning on rocks. I knew it was Lake Meredith again because I'd seen them there.

"Some of these creatures are pets that were released into the wild when they got too big," Pirate Andy said. "This is not a good practice."

He talked about how many of these animals suffer, starve, and die. He also explained how they upset the ecological balance of natural habitats.

"I thought he was going to talk about our mermaid," my mother said.

"Our" mermaid?

"He'll explain," Reggie said, grabbing a cookie.

Next, Pirate Andy was standing on the shore by the bird refuge, throwing feed to them. The camera panned to show the islands in the background, and then the large pen where lots of wild birds that had been injured were kept. There were chickens and several large white geese in the pen among the wild birds. I had seen them of course, and I always wondered why farm animals were in there.

Then the camera cut to a large lawn that was behind a nearby community college. Black-and-white bunnies were eating grass. The person holding the camera started walking toward them. The bunnies all started running away and you could see how many there were.

"These rabbits have successfully learned to survive, to the point that they're proliferating rapidly," Pirate Andy said. The camera turned up to the sky where we saw a hawk flying around over the rabbits. "This attracts predators, who sometimes feed on rare, wild birds in the refuge that we're trying to protect."

Another close up of Pirate Andy looking into the camera. "Is it possible that the person who found the baby mermaid, released her into Lake Meredith when she got too big for a home aquarium?"

I caught my breath and glanced at Reggie and my mom, but their eyes were glued to the screen. Of course, they didn't know *I* was the guilty one. Next, Pirate Andy was at the ranger's station, interviewing the same lady ranger we had talked to.

"No, I haven't seen the mermaid myself, but people have reported seeing something unusual in the lake," she said. "I wasn't convinced until I saw this."

The camera moved up to a large bulletin board with drawings of the lake with a mermaid, done by children. In the very center was a photograph. It was the same one with Kitty, Bambi and me in our mermaid costumes, except it had been blown up, and our faces were blurred out by the camera. I didn't know that Kitty's mother had given a copy to the rangers!

"That's you and your mermaid friends at Halloween!" Reggie shouted. "Isn't that cool?"

No, it wasn't one bit cool.

There was a big red cutout arrow pointing at the spot behind us where Mermary was swimming underwater. Underneath, someone had tacked a sign that read, "CAN YOU SEE THE FOURTH MERMAID?"

When the picture was small, all we could see was Mermary's general shape. In the blown up picture you could see the head, arms, long tail, and fins very clearly, even if it was still just a shadow.

"Looks like a mermaid to me," the ranger said.

I glanced at my mother. She had a look she gets when she knows someone's trying to pull a fast one on her, so I knew she didn't think it was real.

Next, Pirate Andy was in the front of a small motor boat in Lake Meredith. With him was another ranger, this time a man, wearing a hat. They were jetting out over the water. The ranger was talking about sometimes going out to the little islands to check on the birds and make sure everything was all right on the islands. He pulled up to the side of one of the bird islets and idled the engine.

"I noticed this opening some time ago. Natural erosion created this space by washing the dirt away from the tree roots."

We couldn't really see much; it looked like an overhang, with roots from a tree over the water. Then the ranger got a flashlight and shone it up inside. The camera got really close. You could see there were old bottles, corroded utensils, pieces of pottery, mostly broken. They were lined up neatly on shelves that had been fashioned out of mud and boards wedged into roots. There were also two waterlogged dolls, both stained from being in the water. With a shock I realized this was Mermary's cave!

"There wasn't anything inside here the last time I checked, say, six months ago," the Ranger was saying. "No one's allowed on these islands except me. So how could these things have gotten in here? Who could have arranged them like this? I was bamboozled. Then people started talking about the mermaid."

The camera did a close up of him looking really amazed, even scared in a way.

"The mermaid is real," he said.

"There *is* a mermaid cave, just like I figured!" Reggie said excitedly. "We just couldn't see it from where we were!"

Next the camera followed Pirate Andy walking up to a small group of people with signs that said, "Protect our Mermaid!" and "Keep the

Mermaid for Luna Beach!" Others had clipboards, and people were signing it. Pirate Andy asked one of them what it was about.

"We're collecting signatures for laws to protect our mermaid, and so that no one can take her away from Lake Meredith," the spokeswoman said. "We got the idea from Scotland, where they have laws that protect Nessie, the Loch Ness monster."

The pirate turned to face the camera again.

"The Save Our Mermaid group was formed by citizens of Luna Beach because news of the mermaid has begun to attract many people, some from outside of Luna Beach. Some of whom believe she should be in a place where everyone can see her. As it is, she's only been glimpsed in Lake Meredith by less than ten people as far as we know."

Ten people? Had that many people really seen Mermary?

In the next scene, Pirate Andy was walking on a dock to where a man and woman were putting equipment on a boat.

"I understand you're going out to look for the mermaid," Pirate Andy said.

"That's right," the man said. "We have a special sounding instrument that sends back images of what's under the water."

The camera zoomed in on strange looking instrument with lots of dials and buttons and a computer screen. He demonstrated how it worked by putting a funny looking hose down in the water. After a moment a sort of picture turned up on the screen. Even though it was just a line drawing, you could see there was a tire, some cans and bottles, a board and a boot in the water. Then a little fish came into the picture and swam through.

"This is a picture of what's in the water underneath our boat right this very minute," the man said. "This instrument has been used with great success at deep levels in the ocean. Lake Meredith at the deepest point is only thirty feet. If there's a mermaid here, we'll find her."

Pirate Andy looked into the camera. "I'm an experienced scuba diver, and I've gotten special permission from the mayor of Luna Beach to search the waters of Lake Meredith. With me will be two marine scientists who have agreed to help me locate this rumored mermaid."

"What will you do if you find the mermaid?" someone asked him.

"Well, us old Sea Salts have a long history with mermaids. I swear I saw a mermaid once, and I'm determined to see one again. If I find the mermaid, I'm going to catch her if I can. Here in Lake Meredith, she faces danger from pollution and vandals, risks injury from propellers or hooks, and even kidnapping. I know the mermaid will be very happy living at the Marineland Aquarium in southern California. For one, the weather is better there. She'll have a safe place to live, clean water, and plenty of food. She'll also have a team of trained workers to watch over her and tend to her every need."

The screen showed footage of sunny Marineland, with big tanks and seals and killer whales. The Marineland Aquarium was a place for big water shows. I might never see Mermary again! I was so upset I could barely listen to Pirate Andy, who was still talking.

"Keep a look out for my next show, 'The Search for a Mermaid.' This is Pirate Andy Kydd, signing off now."

"Well, this is exciting for Luna Beach, isn't it?" my mother said, smiling.

"It sure is," Reggie said, taking another cookie.

I didn't want any. I felt sick. Holding the cookie in her mouth, Reggie started typing again.

"Let's look at Pirate Andy's mermaid site," she said around the cookie. The web page opened. "I found this website a few months ago." And of course, it was the website I stopped visiting.

"Let me show you the posting Pirate Andy was talking about." She started paging down. I wanted to tell her to stop, I was afraid my mother would guess I had visited the site without her permission.

"Look, here's the posting he was talking about, from someone in Luna Beach." Reggie looked at me. "Do you think Sea Bee is a girl?"

I shrugged and didn't look at Reggie or my mother. Why did Reggie want to know?

I was so relieved when my mother finally said, "All right, girls, if you're finished with the computer, I need to get back to work."

Reggie jumped up from the computer.

"Sooner or later, someone's going to find that mermaid!" she said.

That's what I was afraid of!

CHAPTER 54
A DIRE WARNING

My mother dropped me off at school earlier than usual the next day, and as soon as she was gone I walked all the way to the Dragon Tree. I called Mermary.

"Hi, Camile! How are you?"

"Mermary, you're in danger. People are coming to try and find you. There's going to be divers using scuba gear to search the waters. Some of them are scientists. And others will be using specialized equipment to locate you in the water!"

"Like what?"

"A sounding machine that sends back pictures to a computer of what's in the water."

"Oh, is *that* what those people were doing," she said, almost to herself.

"What people?"

"Well, three people were in a rowboat, and one of them had a long box with glass and a light they put down into the water."

That didn't sound like what I'd seen on Pirate Andy's show. There must be all kinds of equipment people were using to see underwater!

"Did they see you, Mermary?"

"No. I stayed away from the light."

"Were you really close to them?"

"No."

"Maybe you should stay in your cave during the day time."

"Stay in the cave? That's boring!"

"I know, but—" I knew it wasn't a good solution.

"How about if I just stay away from boats. I'll hear when someone's coming, and I'll swim away from them."

"I'm just so worried someone's going to find you some day, then they'll take you away."

"I'll be too fast for them. If they try to catch me in a net, I'll cut my way out," she said, pulling the knife I gave her from its sheath. "And if they try to get me, I'll fight them."

Her saying that only made me more upset, and sad too. She didn't know what some people were like, how they would hunt her until she was caught, and probably use nets made of stuff she couldn't cut through. Her little knife wouldn't help her at all.

"I'm glad you're doing your best to stay away from people. But we have to do something more so they *never* catch you."

"Like what, Cammie?"

"I don't know. I have to figure it out."

CHAPTER 55
WORRY

I thought and I thought for the rest of that week and I still didn't know what to do. Should I just wait to see what happened? Should I trust Mermary to stay hidden and keep away from people? Maybe no one would find her.

But what if they did? I couldn't take that chance.

I was so worried that I couldn't concentrate in school. I got a D on a spelling test even though I'm an excellent speller, and I actually failed a math test. I was too upset to care. I thought of something else: if they caught Mermary, how long would she live in captivity, with so many people gawking at her, and scientists studying her and putting her through tests? Would the scientists *want* her to die, so they could dissect her to see what she was like inside, just like that movie? Mermary would be stressed and miserable, and maybe even get depressed. And it would be my fault, all my fault! I had committed the sin of selfishness.

Twice Sister had to get my attention because I was staring out the window at the lake.

The second time, Jeannie said, "Camile's distracted by the mermaid."

Some of my classmates giggled.

"Have you seen her again?" Emily asked.

Everyone was looking at me, so I shook my head and looked down at my geography book. I was too upset even to feel embarrassed. I felt like crying.

"I bet she has," Allie said. "I wouldn't pay attention to school work either."

Before recess, Sister asked me to remain behind. I figured I was in trouble, and Sister was going to get after me. After the third grade teacher took both classes out to the school yard and I was alone with Sister, she asked me if everything was all right. I nodded, but it wasn't true of course.

"Camile, you're a very bright and gifted student. This is the first time all year you haven't done well. Furthermore, you haven't turned in any homework this week."

"I'm sorry. I'll make it up."

"Dear, I think something's wrong. Can you tell me what it is?" She was being so kind that I started crying. She got a box of tissue and brought it over to me. I grabbed one and covered my face with it.

"Are things all right at home?"

I nodded.

"Is anyone bothering you? Are your classmates teasing you? Maybe about the mermaid?"

I shook my head. Actually, they did tease me, but it was nice teasing. To them, I was like a hero because I had "shown" them the mermaid. But I wasn't a hero. I was a selfish liar. That made me cry even more.

"Has anyone bothered you at the lake?" Sister asked. "A stranger, perhaps?"

I shook my head again. Finally I thought of something I could say that would explain everything. I wiped my eyes.

"I'm worried about the mermaid. I saw a program on pollution, and how it kills fish and animals. I'm afraid that the mermaid might be living in a polluted environment." This wasn't a lie, because I *was* worried about pollution, and worried because Mermary liked to eat the junk food that people threw into the lake.

"Yes, I can see why that would be upsetting," Sister agreed. "And it is a very big problem." She talked some about pollution and suggested some things I could do, like join the town's litter-pickup days. Then she said, "Have you prayed about it, Camile?"

I shook my head. I had been so upset, I never thought about praying.

"Prayer can help ease your soul when you're troubled," she said.

Just thinking about praying helped me to feel a little bit better. I took a breath. "Can I go to the church now?"

She checked her watch. "Yes, of course. I'll take you."

We went over to the church and entered by the side door. It was big and quiet as usual. I knelt down in front of Our Lady of the Lake. Sister knelt down next to me. I prayed a little bit, but mostly I looked up at the Madonna. Even though she was white and polished, she seemed alive. Her pretty face was gentle, and I trusted her.

Please, tell me what to do to protect Mermary, I asked her in silence. I kept staring at her. It almost seemed like she was smiling at me. I felt a lot better. We could hear the students coming in and Sister said it was time to go back to class.

After that I was able to pay attention and not stare at the lake so much. The three o'clock bell rang, and amazingly only Bambi came over to tell me we had to cancel singing practice on Saturday because her grandmother was visiting. Other than that, no one asked me to walk home. I left school and went to Dragon Tree Point. After a moment, Mermary popped up.

"Hi, Cammie! It's nice to see you!"

"Hi, Mermary," I said. "How are you?"

She told me about her day. I told her I'd had a bad week because I was so worried about her, but that I'd prayed and asked Our Lady of the Lake to help us.

"Did she?"

I nodded. What I had to say was very difficult. "Mermary, how would you feel about leaving the lake?"

"Where would I go?"

"Well . . . I think you'll be safer in the ocean."

Mermary leapt and did a somersault in the air. "Yay! I've wanted to go there for so long. I can smell the ocean and feel it, and I've been so curious about it! When? When can I go?"

I was glad that Mermary wouldn't be sad to leave Lake Meredith, although I was sad she wouldn't be near me anymore.

"Soon, I hope," I said. "What I have to figure out, is how."

CHAPTER 56
A SOLUTION COMES IN A DREAM

The next day was Saturday. I woke up and listened to the ocean while I thought about a dream I had. Reggie was in it, and she was wearing a kerchief like a pirate. She was showing me a treasure map and pointing at a trail that was plotted out with dashes across it to a beach.

"We'll keep this a secret," Reggie said.

Then we were floating in the ocean with Mermary. A white mermaid, bigger than a whale, held out her hands while she sang up to the moon. I didn't mind that Reggie could see me with Mermary. I felt really happy.

I always wrote down my dreams about Mermary, so I got out my mermaid journal. After writing my dream, I drew a picture of the giant mermaid. Her curly tail made me think of Our Lady of the Lake. All of a sudden I knew what the dream meant. I had to talk to Reggie.

I got up and put my clothes on. After I fed the fish, I looked out my window. The day was overcast. I put on the pirate girl sweatshirt Reggie had given me. It seemed like a good thing to wear for what was ahead of me.

At breakfast I got permission to spend the day with Reggie. I set out right after I brushed my teeth, not even waiting to call her, and walked to Reggie's house. A breeze was coming off the sea, blowing a few clouds inland. I was glad it wasn't too hot. Reggie opened the door.

"Hi, Cam, what's up?"

"Reggie, I need your help with a secret project. Are you busy? Can we go someplace where no one will hear us?"

"My parents are in the garden and probably won't be in for a while, but we can go up to my room."

On our way up the stairs I looked out the window to make sure her parents were still in the backyard. Her father was digging and her mother was moving plants.

"Is anyone else here?" I asked, because sometimes her brother came home for visits, and I didn't want him surprising us.

"No."

We went into her room and closed the door, then sat in chairs in the little dormer.

"What's going on, Cam, are you in trouble?"

"No. Well, yes, in a way. I made a serious mistake, and now I have to fix it. I had a dream, and you were in it." I told her the dream. "I think the big mermaid was Our Lady of the Lake."

"Sounds like it. Do you think it means anything?"

"Yes. Our Lady of the Lake was telling me you could help me."

"How? And what's the problem?"

"It concerns the mermaid."

Reggie got excited. "Cool! Have you seen her?"

"First, you have to totally promise me you won't tell anyone else. At least, not until after this problem's been fixed."

She promised, but I had kept Mermary a secret for so long, I didn't know how to start talking about her. "I'm sorry, Reggie, but I had to lie to you about the mermaid."

"*What?* You mean there *is* a mermaid at the research center?"

"No, thank goodness," I said. "About the mermaid in Lake Meredith. I told you I didn't know anything about her. But I did. I do."

"What!? Tell me!"

I took a deep breath. "Not only have I seen her, I know her. She's my friend. Her name is Mermary."

Reggie's eyes got big. "You actually know her? You mean, you've talked to her?"

"Yes. In fact, I'm the one who put her in the lake."

"*You* did? Why?!"

"I found her, when she was just a tiny mermaid."

With my fingers, I showed her how big Mermary was then. I told Reggie the whole story, how the storm floods had brought the mermaid to the open drain outside our house; how I kept her in the aquarium in my room, and lived with her for months.

"So that *was* you! On Pirate Andy's website!" she almost shouted.

I nodded.

"That's why I went over to your house the very first time," Reggie said. "I found the posting and I thought Sea Bee might be you. So I went over to your house to see if there was a mermaid, but there wasn't. But it was all just like you posted on Pirate Andy's site: you didn't live far from the ocean, there was an open drain where a mermaid could have lived, and an aquarium, but no mermaid.

"Then I thought maybe your mother took her to the research center, but she wasn't there either. I finally decided you had made it up. I didn't mind, because I make up stuff too."

"You do?"

"Yeah, like when I told you I thought I saw a school of mermaids. It turned out to be just a bunch of seals, but it sounds cooler to say it was mermaids," Reggie said. She thought for a minute. "You know, I thought there was something strange and coincidental about all that."

"About what?"

"Well, when I first heard about the mermaid, I thought she must have got in from the ocean, through the locks at the end of the lake. Then I found that posting. A few months later, all of a sudden everyone's saying there's a mermaid in the lake. It seemed like a coincidence somehow, but I couldn't put it together. But why did you put her there?"

"It was just like Pirate Andy said. I released her into the lake because she was getting too big for the aquarium in my room," I said. "I didn't want to put her in the ocean because she was so small, I was afraid something would eat her. But I also wanted to keep her where I could see her all the time because she was so pretty and wonderful, and . . . and because I didn't have any friends."

My whole face burned as I admitted this, but I was tired of all the lying I'd been doing, and I may as well tell the whole story.

"How come you didn't tell me?" Reggie demanded.

"Because I knew it was better not to tell anyone. It's really hard to keep secrets. I've heard classmates tell secrets when they didn't know I was listening. They would tell the person, 'don't tell anyone,' and then that person would tell someone, and after a while everyone knew.

"For me it was easy not to tell anyone, because it was so hard for me to chat. And I knew I couldn't tell my parents, because they would have taken her away from me."

"Why?"

"Because they're scientists. If marine biologists got their hands on a mermaid, they would never set her free. She would be too valuable a find. My own mother even said so."

"Makes sense," Reggie said. "So tell me about her, how big is she now? What's her name? Can I meet her?"

"Her name is Mermary. I'll tell you everything I know about mermaids," I said. "I'll even show you the journal I kept about her.

Best of all, you'll get to meet her. But first, we have to figure out how we're going to save her."

"From what?"

"From Pirate Andy and his scientists, and all the people we saw in his show who are trying to find Mermary."

"Why? They're not going to hurt her, I don't think."

"We can't take that chance. You saw *Splash*. Remember when they found out Madison was a mermaid, and they locked her in a dark basement laboratory so they could study her, and she got sick and started wasting away?"

"Yes."

"Well, that's real. We can't let that happen to Mermary."

"Oh . . . so you want me to help find a way to keep her hidden?"

"No. I need your help setting her free."

"But she *is* free."

"No. Or rather, she's free right now, but she's a sitting duck in the lake. Sooner or later, someone is going to catch her."

"What can we do?"

"We have to take her to the ocean and set her free there."

"No way!" Reggie said. "It's really cool that Luna Beach has a genuine mermaid!"

"Yes it is, it's the most wonderful thing in the world to me. But it's even more important that she has her freedom."

"But people are making laws to protect her. Remember?"

"No. They're campaigning for laws. My mother explained all this to me. The laws haven't been made yet, it'll take a while. And what if the government decides they want the mermaid? They can probably overrule any local law. We have to save Mermary now, today if possible. Before she's found."

"Today?"

"Yes. It won't be long before Mermary shows up on one of those fancy water computers we saw on the pirate's show, then they'll know for a fact there's a mermaid. Her life is at stake. And even if it isn't, you heard Pirate Andy. His scientist friends are planning to take her away from Luna Beach. Or even worse, the government will seal off the whole lake while they do their experiments, like in that documentary. Then we won't have a mermaid *or* a lake.

"Also, after they finished examining her, and taking samples of her skin and blood and hair and poop, and asking thousands of stupid questions, they'll probably let her waste away and die so they can dissect her and study her insides. We can't let that happen."

I took a deep breath. I had never said so much in my whole life.

"You're right," Reggie said at last.

"So, will you help me figure out how to get her from the lake to the ocean?"

Reggie was quiet while she thought about it. Then she stood up and went to put on one of her pirate T-shirts.

"Of course I'll help you," she said. "That's what friends are for."

I was so grateful, I hugged her.

CHAPTER 57
A SECRET PLAN

"Can we put her in the basket on my bike and take her? I can ride you too."

"She's too big for your basket. Besides, we need to take her in something that holds water so she won't dry out on the trip to the ocean."

"Oh." Reggie thought some more. "How about if we put her in a bucket and take her there? We can take turns carrying her, or carry her between us maybe."

"It would have to be a really big bucket." I told her how heavy Mermary had been when I carried her to the lake, and that she was much bigger now. "Plus, she'll need water to keep her moist, and water is heavy."

"The best thing would be to get someone to drive us there. My mom or dad could drive us to the beach . . . or better yet, my brother? We can trust him. He's coming home in a couple of weeks. He'll help us."

I knew Reggie adored her brother and trusted him completely, but I didn't know what he would do if he found out about the mermaid. He studied computer science, but he was still a scientist.

"We can't wait that long. We have to do it today, if we can. You saw all those people searching Lake Meredith. They're probably looking for her right this minute," I said. "And we can't ask your parents to drive us. They'll want to know what we're doing, and once they see it's a real mermaid, they might not let us set her free."

Reggie thought for a minute. "Let's go see what we have in the basement."

We went down and looked around. It was dark with cement walls and high windows, and the washer and dryer were in there, next to a couple of big sinks.

"Hey, look at this!" Reggie pulled a big, five-gallon plastic bucket out from under one of the sinks. It was full of old rags. She dumped them out. "Is this big enough to hold Mermary?"

"I think so, but with her in it, and water, it will probably be too heavy for us to carry to the ocean. That's the problem."

"Then we need something with wheels . . . we have a wheelbarrow, but my parents are using it today I think. What else . . . ?" She opened the door into the garage. Underneath a work bench along the side was a small wooden platform. She put her foot on it and drew it out. There were wheels on the underside. "My brother uses this to work underneath cars." She set the bucket on it and pushed it. "It's difficult to steer, but it might work with both of us steering it."

I noticed something flat with wheels on the wall of the garage. It was a square wire object.

"What's that?"

Reggie looked where I was pointing. "Hey, I bet that'll work! It's a cart." She took it down and unfolded it. We picked up the bucket and set it down inside. It fit perfectly.

I clapped. "It works!"

We took it out to the front and Reggie got the hose and put water in the bucket.

"How much water do we need, like halfway?"

"No, maybe about an eighth or quarter full."

I wasn't feeling quite so worried anymore. I was sure this would work now. Our plan was coming into place, and Reggie had been exactly the right person to help me after all!

CHAPTER 58
A PLAN IN ACTION

"Is there anything else besides water Mermary will need?"

I was glad Reggie reminded me.

"Something to protect her from the sun would be good," I said.

The clouds were starting to burn off, and it would probably get warmer. I went back into the house and sorted through the rags Reggie had stuffed back under the sink. I found one that would cover the top, but that had a loose weave so Mermary could get air. Then I remembered I had put seaweed into the bucket the first time I transported her. She would need something to hide in, in case someone looked into the bucket. I told Reggie about it.

"I have lots of seaweed at home, but I don't want my mother to know what I'm doing."

"Let's see if there's anything in the compost pile."

Outside, Reggie ran over to where her parents were piling branches and weeds.

"How about these?" Reggie asked, pulling some branches out with dark green leaves and purple berries. She picked some of the berries and ate some, then handed me one.

"They're perfect," I said. "Mermary might even like to snack on the berries."

"Dad," Reggie called. "Is it okay if we take some of these for a nature project Cam is doing?"

I liked that Reggie called it that.

Her dad straightened from where he working in the garden. "Help yourselves."

"Just a few," I told Reggie. "We need to leave plenty of room for Mermary."

We carried them to the front. We put them in the bucket, and they came to a couple of inches over the lip, and we draped the cloth over the whole thing.

Reggie went to tell her parents we were headed off to the lake to complete my "science project." Reggie's mom came out front with her.

"What's your project, Camile?" she asked.

I didn't know what to say.

"We're going to catch the mermaid!" Reggie said.

I thought I was going to faint, but her mother just smiled and kissed her on the cheek.

"Okay. Try to stay out of trouble," she said. "What time will you be home?"

"About three, three-thirty?" Reggie looked at me. It was nearly eleven, I hoped that would give us plenty of time to carry out our plan. She knew what I was thinking and told me, "I have my phone. If we need more time, I'll call and let my parents know."

We started off. I looked back, but her mother was gone.

"Reggie, I can't believe you told your mother the truth."

Reggie just waved her hand. "Oh, I knew she wouldn't believe me. Sometimes the best alibi is the truth."

We set out for the lake, pulling the cart behind us. Reggie was excited.

"I can hardly wait! I'm going to meet a real mermaid!" she said.

I was too stressed to be excited. "We should practice with different ways of pulling the cart."

So we tried going faster and faster and almost knocked the cart over. Then we tried pushing it in front and dragging it behind us, and figured out how to handle it when the sidewalk was broken or uneven, and learned how to let it down gently at curbs. We found a good speed, not too fast and not too slow, pushing it in front of us.

It took about fifteen minutes to get to the lake. A lot of people were gathered around the landing at the colonnade, and we could hear beautiful, tinkling music.

"That's where I used to meet Mermary before school," I told Reggie. It still felt strange to be telling someone about her.

"What's happening over there?" Reggie asked, pointing at all the people. "Let's go see."

We made our way through the crowd and saw there were two women in long, green dresses, playing harps in the middle of the landing. One harp was so big, it stood on the landing. The other musician held a smaller harp in her lap. The music was beautiful, like something fairies would play. In front of them was a sign saying "Marla and Kendra from the Luna Beach Symphony Orchestra." Some people were around them, listening to the music, but several were facing the lake, watching the water.

"What's going on?" Reggie asked an old lady with wire-rimmed glasses and a hat with a big brim.

"They're playing music, hoping to attract the mermaid," the old lady said.

A man leaning against the column rolled his eyes. "I think they're really advertising the symphony." You could tell he didn't believe in mermaids. Mermary loved music and I knew she probably *was* there, listening. I just hoped no one would see her by accident.

"I'm going to let Mermary see me so she'll know we're here," I whispered to Reggie. I went to the side and all around by the edge of the landing, and I stuck my thumb up in the direction we were going to go. She would probably guess I meant Dragon Tree Point. Then I slipped back to Reggie.

"Okay, let's go."

"You saw her?"

"No, but I know she saw me. Come on."

We started pulling the cart away when that bossy girl Helen from my school, came over and stood in front of our cart.

"What does this mean?" she asked. She made the same sign I had made to Mermary. "Is it mermaid for 'come here'?"

I didn't know what to say, I just stood there with my mouth open.

"You were signaling to the mermaid, weren't you," she said. She looked at the cart and bucket. "What are you up to?"

"None of your beeswax," Reggie said. "Who are you, anyway?"

Helen glanced at Reggie, then back at me. "What are you doing with that bucket?" She grabbed the cloth away and looked inside. "Is that what you're feeding the mermaid?"

I just kept staring at her, frozen.

"My brother told me about you," she said.

"Your brother?" I asked.

"Hello-o? Michael Crisp? Your classmate?" Of course, Michael. He had freckles and glasses and black hair, and he was the smartest boy in our class. "He said you're a mermaid expert, and that you come to the lake every day. He didn't know why, but I figured it out. You hang out with the mermaid, don't you?"

I was really scared. She was talking loudly, and people were listening.

"How do you know so much about mermaids?" she demanded.

"I read about them," I said.

"Sure you do," she said. "You better tell me about that mermaid."

Reggie butted in. "What are you, eleven?"

Helen looked offended. "I'm almost thirteen. Why?"

"Aren't you a little old to believe in mermaids? I bet you still believe in the Easter Bunny and Santie Claus."

"I do not."

"Come on," Reggie said to me, grabbing the cloth back from Helen. "We have to get these cuttings home to my parents." She pushed Helen out of the way and we pulled the cart after us.

"What a nosy girl," Reggie said. "How do you know her?"

"She's some brat from my school," I said.

"*You're* the brat," we heard Helen say and Reggie snickered nastily.

We started heading in the direction of Dragon Tree Point, but I looked back and saw Helen was watching us.

"We can't go to the other place I meet Mermary because that girl is still watching us."

Reggie didn't look back, just kept walking and pushing the cart. "Then we'll keep walking and find another place. Don't look back anymore. Don't even look at the lake. It makes us look guilty."

So we kept walking and didn't go to Dragon Tree Point at all, but cut across the grass to the pathway that ran alongside the lake. I made the signal for Mermary to follow. We passed the Point.

"This wouldn't have been a good place to get Mermary anyway. It's too high off the water. We need a place where we can get down to the water, but where no one can see us."

"Hmmm," Reggie said. "Let me think where would be a good place." So we walked along and were quiet.

"I know where we can go," Reggie said. "You know that beach, where they have that big, yellow sculpture kids climb around on?"

"You mean The Monster? But that area is wide open. People will see us."

"No, next to that. The trees grow down to the lake and hang over the water. I used to play hide and seek there with my brother. The trees will provide cover from all directions."

She was right, that was a great idea. We continued walking on past the ranger's building, then past the bird sanctuary area. I didn't look back anymore, even though it was really hard. But Reggie was right, it would make us look guilty.

There were a lot of people everywhere because it was turning out to be a nice day. I was so glad Reggie was helping me. She was smart and brave, plus she knew how to talk to people like Helen. All of a sudden Reggie stopped.

"Let's get some hotdogs," she said as we reached the concession stand behind the boathouse. I looked at her.

"Are you serious?" I asked. I was too anxious to eat. I just wanted our "science project" to be over with.

"I have a reason," she said. "I'll get hotdogs. You stay with the cart."

She got in line and bought two hotdogs. She put mustard and catsup on hers. "What do you want on yours?" she called over to me.

"I'm not hungry," I said.

"Just mustard?" She acted as if she hadn't heard me and put mustard on the second hot dog. Then she came over to me. "Let's sit up there."

She pointed at the same bench we had sat on when we had our excursion several weeks ago. It was up a little rise. From there we had a view of the lake, the back of the boathouse which was in front of us, and the bird sanctuary on our left. She told me where to sit, then sat on the opposite end of the bench so she was facing the way we had just come.

"Okay, just act normal, and don't look back, no matter what. Just look at me." She started eating her hotdog and talking with her mouth full.

"Blah, blah, blah, blah," she said, and turned her head this way and that. And pointing out at the lake. I looked where she was pointing, but I didn't know why she was pointing. "At least pretend to eat your hotdog."

I took a bite. What in the world was Reggie doing? She finished her hotdog.

"I thought so," she said, leaning back and stretching her arms out across the back of the bench to get some sun.

"What?" I asked.

"I'll tell you, but don't look around, okay? Just keep your head turned this way . . . that girl's following us. What's her name, Hellish? Right now she's by the bird pen, pretending like she's looking at the birds, but she's got her eye on us."

"Oh no. What are we going to do?"

"We just have to wait her out."

Reggie went to get a soft drink and I ate the rest of my hot dog. I didn't look back at all. Reggie shared her soft drink with me. We must have wasted at least twenty minutes.

"I think she's gone," Reggie said. "I saw her walking back the way we came a few minutes ago, but she could be trying to trick us." She threw our trash in a receptacle and looked around. "We're going to make a detour, just in case. Come on, this way."

She headed up a path away from the lake, to a section of the park that was gated. Inside was a big garden area, with different areas like a Japanese garden, a cactus garden, an herb garden, and several vegetable patches where people were working. We went over there.

"My mother brought me here a few times. She gets cuttings, or asks for gardening advice, so I know some of the people here. You watch the gate for old what's her name."

Reggie talked to some of the gardeners. A nice old man gave us kale and collards. I stood across from Reggie and faced the gate, keeping watch for Helen.

"Is she back there?" Reggie asked.

I shook my head.

She turned to take a long look. "Okay, let's go."

But instead of going out the way we came in, she headed through the garden plots to the back of the fenced area, where there was a gardeners' building. On the side of it was a big yard with vehicles that had the city logo, and at the far end was another entrance where cars came and went.

"We're going out this way," Reggie said. "So if Helen is hiding, we can give her the slip."

We got to the back entrance, stuck our heads out, and looked around. There weren't very many people. There was a wide open space with a road. On the far side there were trees that hid the lake from view. Reggie pointed to the right of us.

"Okay. The beach and that yellow sculpture are over to the right, down beyond those trees. Our destination is there," she said, pointing directly across from us. "There's a path that runs along the edge of the trees. We're going over there, and then climb down the side to the water. We're almost there. Here's the thing, Cam. It'll take us a minute to cross, and we won't have any cover. We'll be sitting ducks if Helen comes around that corner. If that happens, we'll have to give up for today."

My shoulders slumped. I didn't think I could wait another week.

"It's okay, Cam. If that happens, just think of today as a practice run. Are you ready?"

I closed my eyes and said a prayer to Our Lady of the Lake. It made me feel like I had more courage, so I nodded.

"Okay, let's go."

We headed out the back gate and crossed the road and over the grass to the trees.

"Is it okay if I look?" I asked.

"Yeah, it doesn't matter now."

I didn't see Helen.

We made it to the path next to the trees. We checked for Helen one last time, but still didn't see her.

"Okay, this is it," Reggie said.

We started making our way down through the trees and bushes to the lake. We had to lift and carry the cart. Reggie got at the bottom and I held the handle. About halfway down I stopped. The trees and shrubs were pretty thick, so I didn't think anyone would be able to see us from the path above. Reggie had been right, it was a perfect spot.

"Wait here," I told Reggie. "Mermary won't come out unless I tell her it's safe. Keep watch, and let me know if anyone's coming. I'll call you when it's okay."

"All right," Reggie said. "If anyone comes, I'll whistle like a bird."

Reggie sat down next to the cart to wait.

CHAPTER 59
HER LAST MOMENTS IN THE LAKE

I made my way down to the water and then continued a little ways away from where Reggie was. I looked around. There were people on the far side of the lake, and some people on a gondola but they weren't looking our way at all. I took a breath and sang the two-note call and waited a few minutes. It seemed to take forever and I started worrying, but finally the water stirred and Mermary surfaced.

"Hi, Cammie! I saw you down by the music and followed like you signaled me to, then I wondered where you were. Is that your friend Reggie with you?"

"Yes. I had to tell her about you. Our Lady of the Lake sent me a dream and told me Reggie would help me get you to the ocean. "

"You're taking me to the ocean? Today?"

I nodded, because a lump was forming in my throat.

"Yeay!" she said. She leapt out of the water and did a somersault in the air. She surfaced again and said, "Can we go now?"

I nodded again. Tears were coming up, but Mermary didn't notice because she was leaping and swimming in fast circles excitedly.

"I can't wait! I can't wait!" she said.

I couldn't remember ever seeing her so happy. I had to be brave, and I reminded myself the ocean was where she belonged.

"Let's go meet Reggie now, okay?" I said, finally.

I made my way back to where Reggie was, halfway down the incline. "You can come down now, Reggie. Bring the bucket."

Reggie took the bucket out of the cart and climbed the rest of the way down to the water. I called Mermary. She popped up.

"Hello, Reggie!" she said. "Camile told me all about you."

"Wow," Reggie said. Her eyes were big as sand dollars. "I mean, hello Mermary!" She squatted down by the water's edge. "A real mermaid!"

"Another person!" Mermary said, and we all laughed.

Reggie held out her hand. Mermary reached out and grasped two of Reggie's fingers. "Hey, she's got three fingers! No wonder you drew mermaids like that."

I nodded. "When I teach people how to draw mermaids, I tell them mermaids only need three fingers. I never told them how I knew that, and no one ever asked."

Mermary dove into the lake, and after a couple of minutes she came up and gave Reggie a spoon. It was old and crusted from being in the lake a long time, but you could still see the unusual shape of the bowl part and flowers on the handle.

"Mermary finds lots of things at the bottom of the lake," I said. "You know my collection of old bottles and stuff in my room? Mermary found them in the lake."

"Wow," Reggie said again. "Thank you, Mermary!"

She asked her lots of questions. Then she got a stick and held it parallel to the water.

"Mermary, can you jump over this?"

Mermary jumped over it easily. Reggie moved the stick higher and higher for Mermary to jump. She loved it. I hadn't known Mermary could jump so high. I wished we could hang out and play for hours, and that the day would never end.

"Mermary, are you ready to get into the bucket and go to the ocean?" I asked.

"Yes! Yes! I can't wait!"

"Do you need to get anything from your cave?"

She shook her head. She was wearing the knife I had given her, and she certainly didn't need to take any of the junk she had in there. I took the vegetables and branches out, and we tipped the bucket most of the way sideways. Mermary leapt in and splashed in the water. She was so long now, she had to draw her tail in the rest of the way.

"Hey," Reggie said. "She has that knife you bought, the one you said was for your mother."

"Sorry, I fibbed about that too," I said. "At least I won't have to lie anymore. I was lying all the time to protect Mermary."

"It's okay. I totally get why you had to do it."

Mermary curled her tail up so it fit in the bottom of the bucket. She kept leaping up and pulling herself up on the side of the bucket, all the way to her waist so she could see out.

"Mermary, you're too visible that way. Stay down. We have plants to help disguise you, in case anyone looks in," I said.

Reggie and I tucked the branches and vegetables around her.

"Are you comfortable, little mermaid?" Reggie asked.

"Yes, let's go! Let's go to the ocean!" she sang.

"Aren't you sad to be leaving the lake?" I asked.

"Sad? Why? It will always be here, and I'll always remember it."

But I didn't know how to explain sadness. I just put the cloth over the branches and the top of the bucket. The bucket was much heavier now, of course. Together Reggie and I lifted it a few feet then set it down to rest, and bit by bit, we got to the trail at the top of the little rise. Before coming out of the bushes, we checked to see if Helen was nearby. There were a few other people around, but no Helen.

"Wait with Mermary, I'll get the cart," I said.

I dragged it up the rest of the way and back onto the path. We both lifted the bucket inside, and I covered the top of the branches with the cloth. Finally we were ready for the last and most difficult part of the journey.

CHAPTER 60
JOURNEY TO THE BEACH

We started pushing the cart toward the park exit. Mermary jumped up the side of the bucket and pulled on the rag, clinging to the edge with her little hands and looking over the side.

"I want to watch where we're going!" she said.

"But someone might see you!" I said anxiously.

"No they won't. I'll see them first, and I'll duck and hide."

"Here," Reggie said. We stopped and she arranged the branches at the sides of the bucket, draped the rag over them, then folded back the rag so it made a little doorway so Mermary could see out. We passed a lot of people and each time, Mermary disappeared like she said she would, but hardly anyone looked at the cart or bucket. We reached the sidewalk outside the park and stopped for a rest.

"It's that way, that way!" Mermary cried, pointing toward the ocean.

"You're right," Reggie said. "That's west, and that's where the beach is."

Then she told her each of the directions, pointing so Mermary would know which was which.

"I know the directions in my body," Mermary said. "I can feel them. Now I know what they're called."

That was something else I could put in my mermaid journal. Probably the last thing.

Reggie looked at me. "I guess it's about one good mile to the ocean." She looked at her phone. "It's after one. This will probably take an hour. Are you ready?"

She was asking me, but Mermary said, "Yes! Yes! I'm ready!"

I nodded and didn't look at Reggie because the knot was back in my throat. We started off. Mermary kept asking "what's that?" and Reggie and I would tell her. We passed people with baby carriages, lots of bicyclists, and a man in a wheelchair. Each time we pulled to the side to let them pass so we wouldn't draw attention to ourselves. That slowed us up some, but I didn't mind. We were really careful when we crossed streets, especially the busy ones. I saw some kids from school across the boulevard and we waved at each other, but I worried about running into someone we knew on our same side. They would probably want to know what was in the bucket. If they did, I hoped they wouldn't look too carefully.

Mermary munched on the vegetables and berries in the bucket. Reggie kept asking her if she was okay, if she needed anything, and pointing out sights of interest to her, like a funny looking bald dog and a Model T car. Mermary splashed water on herself now and then.

"Cool!" Reggie said, watching her. "I still can't believe I'm seeing a real mermaid."

I was still afraid Helen might be following us. What would happen if we made it all the way to the beach, and it turned out she was following us the whole time? Reggie noticed.

"Why do you keep looking back?"

"I'm worried that girl is following us."

"Don't be. What's she going to do now?"

"She might stop us from releasing Mermary!"

"How is she going to do that?"

"She might tell someone."

"No one will believe her," Reggie said.

"What if she takes the bucket away from us?"

Reggie thought about that as she looked all around.

"I'm pretty sure she's not back there, Cam. Anyway, we can't worry about that. We just have to move forward and deal with whatever happens when it comes up."

"Don't worry, Camile," Mermary said. "I'll hide so well, she won't be able to see me. There's lots of branches in here."

Finally I said okay and we continued on our journey. It took a long time to get to the ocean. I was sure it was more than a mile, plus we had to stop and rest several times. Sometimes Mermary would sing. Reggie was amazed at everything Mermary did. I was used to her, so I liked seeing Reggie be amazed for the first time.

At last we reached the boardwalk and the beach. Reggie and I stood looking out at the ocean while we rested one more time.

"The ocean! The ocean!" Mermary cried, pulling herself up high on the edge and even kneeling on it, or at least bending her tail so it looked like kneeling.

"Careful, Mermary!" I said. "Don't fall out!"

"I won't," she assured me. "I have excellent balance."

A wind was blowing fog in and the day was cooling. Aside from us, there were only about three people walking on the beach, and they were far away. I was tired, but we were almost done, and best of all, we hadn't been caught. But the part I dreaded most had come.

"This is the hardest part," I said.

Reggie nodded. "I wish there was another way."

"The only way would be to give her to my mother. I can't do that."

Reggie nodded again. "I know." It looked like her eyes were wet too.

I took a deep breath. "Let's go," I said bravely.

We started lowering the cart down to the sand. Mermary perched on the edge of the bucket and did something I never heard her do before. She cheered with a strange and beautiful cry that sounded incredibly happy. Reggie and I looked at each other.

"Wow," Reggie said. "That is totally awesome."

As sad as I was, her cry told me this was absolutely the right thing to do. We were bringing Mermary to her true home.

"I can taste the ocean!" Mermary told us.

We started pulling the cart across the sand but the wheels sank, so we had to drag the whole thing at an angle. Mermary raised herself on the edge so she could see the water.

"My new home!" she said. She climbed part way out of the bucket.

"Mermary, stop! If you fall out, you'll land on dry sand!"

"So?" she said. "I'll just wash it off in the ocean!" But she settled back along the side and rested her head on her folded arms, staring at the waves.

Finally we reached the wet sand. Mermary didn't wait for us to pour her into the ocean. She leapt out and scurried to the water's edge and dove in.

"Mermary!" I screamed.

She came back out, washed up in the next wave.

"What's wrong?" she asked.

I didn't know what to say. She was where she needed to be and my part was done. I walked up close to her and knelt down in front of her.

"Aren't you going to say good-bye?" What I really wanted was for her to stay with us for a while before leaving, but I could tell she was very impatient to be in the ocean.

"Oh, I wasn't leaving yet. I was just trying out the water." She dove in again and I watched anxiously. She came out again, then dove into the water again several more times, taking longer to come back each time.

"This is wonderful!" she cried. "The water is alive!" She burrowed into the wet sand and came up with a sand crab, its little whitish-grey legs waving in the air.

"Look at what I found!" She set it down and it immediately disappeared down in the sand. Mermary looked surprised. Reggie and I both laughed. Mermary dove into a wave, and after a minute, she came out with a ribbon of seaweed. She wrapped it around herself and dove in again.

She came out again and the seaweed was gone. She slithered all the way up to me, where I stood away from the edge of the water.

"I'm ready to go now, Cammie," she said.

I nodded. I was biting my lips.

"Good bye, Camile," Mermary said. "Thank you for bringing me here."

I was trying really hard not to cry. I crouched down and kissed her, even though my sneakers and jeans got wet. "Mermary, please be really careful. Stay away from big fish until you know what they are, and that they're not going to eat you. You'll know because you'll see them eating fish your size."

Of course, that was probably most of the fish in the sea. I tried not to think about that.

"I will." She promised. She kept turning to look at the water.

"I love you, Mermary," I said, starting to cry. "I love you so much."

She took my hand. "I love you too, Cammie."

"Do you?"

"Of course. How could I not love you? You saved me, and have taken really good care of me. You're pretty, and smart, and fun. I'll always remember you. Thanks for giving me a really good life." She looked at Reggie. "I'm so glad I got to meet you. You're really kind. I'm glad you're Camile's friend."

"I loved meeting you too, Mermary, little mermaid," Reggie said. "I hope you find your mermaid family."

She held out her hand again and Mermary took it. She leaned over and kissed Mermary on top of her head. Reggie had tears in her eyes too.

"Don't be sad," Mermary said. "This is where I want and need to be, more than any place in the world."

"I know. I'm just sad because I'm afraid for you," I said.

"Don't worry. I have my knife, and I'm really fast."

"And . . . and I'm sad because I'm never going to see you again," I said, and then I did cry.

"I can come back," Mermary said. "How about if I come back in a year?" She looked around. "I can meet you over at those rocks." She pointed at an outcropping of rocks.

A year! A whole year! I nodded, because I couldn't talk anymore.

"Good bye then, Camile and Reggie!"

Mermary blew us kisses, then turned and dove into the ocean. She was gone.

CHAPTER 61
A LONG FAREWELL

I sat on the beach with Reggie, crying. I kept searching the ocean, as if I would see Mermary leaping through the waves.

"It's almost three," Reggie said finally. "We should get back home."

I nodded and forced myself to get up. We dragged the cart and bucket back out to the street. I took one last look at the ocean before we lifted the cart to the boardwalk.

"Why don't we go back to my house?" Reggie asked. "If you go home now, your mother will see your eyes are all red and puffy and want to know why. Have dinner at my house."

So we headed over to Reggie's. We went a lot faster now that the bucket wasn't carrying water or Mermary, but my heart was heavy. On the way, Reggie asked lots of questions, and it was such a relief to finally be able to talk about Mermary.

At Reggie's house I washed my face with cold water and called my mother. After dinner Reggie got out an old videotape with the title, *The Mermaids of Tiburon.*

"I found it among my mom's old videocassettes," Reggie said. "I saved it so we could watch it together."

It was a movie about beautiful mermaids living in an island lagoon in the Mexican ocean. They protected a bed of giant clamshells, and an evil scientist was trying to steal their pearls by blowing up the sea beds with dynamite. A nice scientist was trying to protect the mermaids and their habitat, and in the end he won. I felt a lot better.

Later, when my mother was on her way to pick me up, I asked Reggie what she was going to tell Zander and Elmo about Mermary. It didn't matter who knew now, because Mermary was safe—at least, as safe as she could be in the big, wide ocean.

Reggie shrugged. "Nothing, I guess. They probably wouldn't believe me anyway. At least Zander won't, even if I showed them the pictures."

"What pictures?"

She took out her phone and showed me. She had three photos of Mermary. The first one she was leaping into the bucket, and part of me from behind was in the picture too. The second was really cute, with Mermary holding onto the side of the bucket and looking over the edge of the bucket at Reggie, her head cocked. The last one was of Mermary, washing back to shore. I was in that picture too, crouched down and holding my hand out to her.

"When did you take them?"

"When you weren't looking. I figured if we had to set her free, we should at least keep some pictures. I hope that's okay."

"Of course it is," I said, and I hugged her.

I was so glad she had them. I had never thought about taking pictures of Mermary, and anyway, my cell phone was only for emergencies. I was so glad Reggie had thought of it. It was a way of always having Mermary with me.

CHAPTER 62
THE REST OF THE SCHOOL YEAR

I brought my grades back up and did okay for the rest of the school year. I didn't go to the lake anymore because I missed Mermary, and it made me too sad. I still read books about mermaids whenever I found new ones. Some were adult books. Kids at school still called me the Mermaid Girl.

People kept trying to find the mermaid, and several claimed to have seen her even after she was gone. Other pictures that looked sort of like a mermaid turned up on the ranger's exhibit, including a couple that were obviously fake, but none were as realistic as the photo Kitty's mother had given them.

Although I no longer had to deny I'd seen "the mermaid," I didn't tell anyone else about Mermary. I realized people would be really mad if they learned I had taken her away from the lake, even if I explained why. The only difference was now, when people asked if I had seen her, I said yes, that I had seen her on the first day of school, and I went to the lake every day after that, hoping I'd see her again. I also told them that was what started my interest in mermaids. The only strange thing was that some people didn't believe me. They said I was making it up. I would just shrug and wonder why they had asked me.

Sometimes I dreamed of Mermary. She would be living in my aquarium again, or I would look and she would be with me and my friends. Sometimes I would be swimming with her. Those dreams were so real I'd wake up crying, missing and longing for her.

Kitty and Bambi are still my friends. We talk about mermaids in general and watch movies about them together. But we have other interests too, like choral. I've made friends with other girls in my school too.

Reggie is still my best friend forever. She loves hearing my stories about Mermary, even when I tell them a second or third time. I shared my mermaid journal with her. She drew a comic strip about us taking Mermary to the beach and added lots of adventures we didn't really have. I loved reading them.

She told her brother about Mermary, which I knew she would sooner or later. He never said anything about it, but I would see him looking at me curiously sometimes, like he wasn't sure what to make of it all.

Once when Zander and Reggie were arguing about the existence of mermaids she got so angry, she turned to me. "Can I show him the pictures?" I froze for a minute, but finally I nodded. Zander just laughed when she showed him her phone.

"Those are so-o-o-o fake. I bet if I did a search, I'd find them on the Internet."

"They're not fake," Reggie snapped. "How would I get them from the Internet onto my phone? It doesn't work that way."

"If she was real, why didn't you show her to me?"

Elmo stared at the pictures for a long time and asked a lot of questions, like "she was in a bucket? You transported her in a cart? So she was about a yard long? How big were her hands?" It turned out he was glad that mermaids were so small. "That way they won't be able to get us. Did you know that mermaids have pitchforks?"

"Those are called tridents," I said.

"They also have knives and spears," Reggie said, giving me a knowing look.

A couple of times for special occasions, I was asked to tell mermaid stories to the lower classes or at the library, and once for a big group of kids at Children's Hospital. It was easier telling stories to younger children, still, I was glad for all the practice Sister gave us in public speaking.

CHAPTER 63
TALENT SHOW

At the end of the school year, Bambi and Kitty and I wore our costumes and performed "Under the Sea" at the school talent show. I had maracas, Bambi castanets, and Kitty had a kalimba. We played along with a karaoke version of the song. There was one part where we did a conga line dance Kitty's mother had taught us. The school loved us.

The whole talent show got to perform a second time in the evening for families and friends. When it was over, everyone met in the courtyard next to the school. It was a beautiful, warm evening, and people were pouring out of the auditorium, milling around, saying hello, and talking; some people congratulated us. All of a sudden Helen was in front of me. She put her hands on her hips.

"Why don't you go to the lake anymore, *Mermaid Girl?*" she demanded.

I just looked at her and didn't say anything. I didn't have to answer her questions. Lots of times people are bullies because they know how to scare people. But now that Mermary was safely in the ocean, Helen could do or say anything she wanted to me.

"It's because she isn't there anymore, is she?" Helen said knowingly. I still didn't say anything. "You did something with her, didn't you?" she pressed. People were looking at us now.

"Why do you say that?" I asked. I always wondered if she had seen something because she was so suspicious, but she didn't answer.

"I knew I should have stuck with you that day. Where did you take her?"

"What's she talking about?" Bambi asked me.

"I don't know."

"Yes you do," Helen said, not taking her eyes off me. "I saw you at the lake on the first day of school. You were talking to someone."

I bit my lips, not sure what to say.

"You used to go to the lake twice, every day," Helen went on, not caring who else heard. "On top of that, you're a big mermaid expert. Only now you don't go to the lake anymore. That's because you know the mermaid's not there." She looked at all of us. "So what happened to her?"

Kitty and Bambi looked from Helen to me.

I rolled my eyes at them. "She likes to pick on me about the mermaid."

Kitty got in Helen's face. "Camile didn't do anything to the mermaid. She would never hurt her. She took us over to the lake and showed her to us."

"What?" Helen said. "You actually saw the mermaid?"

"Yes we did. She came when Camile called her! Just ask any girl in our class!"

"When exactly was this?"

I thought Bambi might actually be making things worse, but right then Helen's brother Michael elbowed her out of the way.

"Just ignore her, she's a pain," he said. "Her and her mermaid conspiracy theories." Then he put his arms around me and Bambi and Kitty and gave us a group hug.

"You guys were beautiful. Which one of you wants to marry me?" he asked, and we all giggled.

I saw Reggie heading over with Elmo and Zander and our mothers behind them.

"You guys were great!" she said.

"Oh, and here's the other mermaid kidnapper," Helen said.

"*You* again," Reggie said. "You're still talking about mermaids?" She sounded disgusted and totally believable. "Anyway, why don't you hang out with people your own age? Go kiss a boy, or put on some makeup. You need it."

Helen crossed her arms over her chest and glared at us. The thing was, she had totally been right about everything, but no one would listen to her. It reminded me of that Greek prophet who no one believed, even though everything she said turned out to be true. I had realized sometimes the truth was secondary in importance. People believed what they wanted to believe.

We stayed about half an hour, and as we were leaving, I noticed Helen over at the lake, on the landing where I always used to go. She was searching the water, so I knew she was looking for the mermaid. Her being so mean and accusatory was just about wanting so badly to see the mermaid. I felt sorry for her, because I knew bullies were lonely. Even her own brother didn't like her.

CHAPTER 64
A YEAR GOES BY

I had marked the day that we had set Mermary free on the calendar so I would know when I would see her again. As if I'd ever forget. The night before, I spent at Reggie's house so her parents could take us to the beach. I wanted to go early in the morning, but it was warm and Reggie thought Mermary probably wouldn't come in the daytime because a lot of people would be at the beach.

It was hard waiting all day, plus I worried that Mermary would think I had forgotten or something. Finally after dinner, Reggie asked her mother to take us to the beach so we could look at tide pools. I couldn't ask my mother because she would want to make it a teaching experience and come with us out to the rocks. I knew Mermary wouldn't come out of the water if my mother was there.

While her mom and dad walked on the beach, Reggie and I went out to the rocky part. I was ahead of Reggie, climbing faster because I was so anxious and excited. I stopped two or three times to sing our two-note code. At first I thought no one was there, and Mermary hadn't come. Then I heard the two-note code in beautiful tones sung back to me. I turned in the direction of the singing.

"Mermary!" I said, even though I couldn't see her.

"Hi, Camile!"

I realized I was looking right at Mermary, sitting between rocks, looking almost like one herself, with part of her long tail wrapped around them. She was so much bigger, and her color nearly matched the rocks so it was hard to see her.

I scrambled the rest of the way to her and grabbed her and we hugged each other. That's how large she had grown. Her hair had grown thicker and become more olive colored; it looked like kelp. Her tail half looked tougher, which she would probably need in the ocean. She was so beautiful. Not in a human way, or like the mermaids in paintings, but in a water creature way. I was crying and laughing at the same time. She still wore the knife I had given her, only on a chain belt now. She also had a bag on a strap over her shoulder, and she wore a couple of necklaces.

"Reggie's here too."

"I saw her," she said. Her voice was deeper now. Reggie was still making her way over the slippery rocks. "You two have gotten so big!"

"So have you." I laughed. "How is it living in the ocean?"

"Oh, Camile, I love it so much. It's such a wonderful, beautiful, wild place. Thank you so much for bringing me."

"Is it too cold?"

"I supposed, but it doesn't bother me."

"Is it dangerous?" Reggie asked. "That's what we were mostly worried about."

"Yes, I have to be on the lookout all the time. But most important, I found my people!" she said.

"Other mermaids?" I asked.

"Yes!"

"Lots of them?" Reggie asked.

"Lots of us! We call ourselves the Sea Kin. After I left you, I was alone for about a month, swimming around and getting familiar with the ocean. Any time I saw a big fish, I zipped down to the bottom of the ocean to hide.

"Then one day I heard beautiful underwater calling that was different from the sounds dolphins and whales make. I swam toward the sound. I was so amazed, because all of a sudden I found myself in a gathering of other mer people, females and males! They were surprised to see me too, because they didn't know me.

"We sing to locate each other over distances underwater, like whales and dolphins do, but we also have our own language. I can speak it now, but there are still a lot of words I'm learning. A few of us know some English, but I'm the only one who can read. We also talk to dolphins and whales, and sometimes we help each other. Did you know that they're just as intelligent as we are?"

"Hey, Mermary," Reggie interrupted. "Do you ever find sunken ships on the ocean floor?"

"Yes, and not just sunken ships, but treasure! Oh—" Mermary opened her pouch. "I brought gifts for you." She gave me a ring and an unusual shell that was very flat, with spines around the edge. She gave Reggie a large old button and an ancient coin.

"Wow!" Reggie said. "A gold pieces of eight!"

Both of our gifts had encrusted white crud on them and other discoloration, probably from being under water. I thanked her and put the ring in my pocket so I wouldn't lose it. I was too excited to look at it.

"I found the button and the coin among the bones in the bottom of a galleon. The Sea Kin told me the human it came from was the captain of a pirate ship. They even told me how that ship sank."

"Is that also where you got your necklaces?" I asked.

Mermary had one necklace with large green gemstones that shone out between the corrosion that grew on metal in salt water. The other was a heavy golden chain with a locket on it that looked rusted shut. They looked beautiful on her, and exactly like something a mermaid would wear.

"From other sunken ships," she said. "But there are all kinds of things to find on the ocean floor. The Sea Kin think I'm funny because I like to look for things. They only want useful stuff like spears or rope. But I think of it like when you and your mother would find interesting things in thrift stores."

"We have a present for you too," I said.

"Do you need another knife?" Reggie asked, spoiling the surprise, but we were both too excited to mind.

We opened Reggie's knapsack and brought out a large diver's knife in a leather sheaf we had found at a garage sale and put our money together to buy. She loved it. It fit perfectly in her hand although it looked a little large for her, but I knew it wouldn't be as heavy in the water. Also, there were finger holes along the shaft.

"Those are for your fingers, so you won't drop the knife underwater," Reggie said unnecessarily, because of course, Mermary's fingers slid right into them, and the webbing between her fingers stretched and didn't seem to bother her. "We also got you a sharpening stone." Reggie fished it out of the knapsack and showed her how to use it. That had been Reggie's idea, because she thought it would be better than sharpening tools on rocks.

"What do the Sea Kin do?" I asked.

"Well, we spend most of our time gathering and preparing food—there are so many amazing things to eat in the ocean. We also make a lot of things that we need, like hammocks, or bags like this one—" She patted the one she wore. "But our most important pastime is storytelling. Some of the stories are incredible. We have excellent memories. That's how we pass down our history. We even have ancient stories about when we lived alongside humans."

"You do?"

"Yes. Thousands of years ago we all lived peaceably, but then humans started catching Sea Kin and forcing them to do things for them, or killing us for no reason, or taking us out of the water to live in captivity. The Sea Kin went to war with humans. I'm sorry to say we killed people and sank ships. They're sorry about it too, especially because they learned war isn't a solution, there are just more people and Sea Kin dead. In the end the Sea Kin decided the answer was to stay far away from humans. They believed people would eventually forget there had ever been mermaids.

"They were worried when I told them about all the mermaid paintings and stories people have. They didn't know we're still on human's minds. But I told them in spite of that, most humans don't believe in mermaids, that they think mermaids are legendary. Human children are the only ones who believe in them.

"But that's sad," Mermary went on. "I have so many other fun things to talk about. I've been teaching them all the things I learned from you. Also, I'm their favorite storyteller. A lot of the stories I tell make them laugh. Guess which one they think is the funniest? *The Little Mermaid* story, where Ariel the mermaid wants to be human, and falls in love with a human man!"

"Why do they think that's funny?" I asked.

"Because a mermaid would never be that silly. A Sea Kin female wouldn't marry a human, or give up her tail to have legs and live on land."

"I get it," Reggie said to me. "I read a story once about a man who married a woman, who turned out to be donkey. It was hilarious!"

"We have stories about people trying to live with mermaids, but our stories are tragic," Mermary said. "In the end, the human always drowns, or has to give up his relationship because it never works.

"Since I went to live with them, we now have a story about a girl who saved a mermaid and protected her from other humans until she could set her free to find her family. That's our story of course," Mermary said, smiling at me.

"Really?" I said bashfully. "Do they like that story?"

"They love it! I've told them all about you and the different places I lived, and the long and dangerous trip over land to the ocean, when you and Reggie set me free, rather than allow wicked scientists to capture me and find out mermaids are real. They're amazed that a human child knew better than to let other humans find out about me.

"Living in the sea is such a wonder, and it's so different everywhere we go, with so many different and amazing kinds of fish and other sea creatures. And we meet other Sea Kin too. There are many different kinds of mermaids. I mean, they don't always look like us. Some have five fingers, like people."

So my theory had been right, there *were* different races of mermaids!

"Later this year we'll be migrating to the Indian Ocean. Each place we go there's a large, underwater cavern, hidden lagoon, or uninhabited island where we stay, where humans have never been.

"We always know when humans are around. We can hear and smell them from a long way away, or we hear dolphins and whales talking about people heading our way. If they come into our territory, we leave, no matter what we're doing, and we make sure to take all our things with us so there's no sign of mermaid life. We take no chances that a human will find us. They only allowed me to come today because you two are our heroines."

"What about your mother, did you find her?" Reggie asked.

"No, but the way Sea Kin children are born and raised, it doesn't matter who our mother is. We don't have orphans, because everyone who is old enough is our mother, and all the males who are old enough are fathers. They can't believe that humans reject orphans unless someone chooses one for their family. The Sea Kin believe humans are cruel and thoughtless. They didn't know what to think when I told them how wonderful you are. Now tell me what you two have been doing!"

I told her about our talent show and going into a new grade, and Reggie told her about going on vacation to Yosemite, but our stories didn't seem nearly as interesting as Mermary's. We talked for a long time, when all of a sudden Mermary turned her head toward the ocean. It seemed like she was listening, although I couldn't hear anything. She turned back to us.

"Camile, Reggie, the mer people are calling me. We've stayed in this locale a little longer than we wanted because I told them I had to come back and see you. But now I have to go."

Tears welled up and I couldn't say anything. I hugged Mermary and we kissed goodbye. She hugged and kissed Reggie too. Then in a flash, she slithered over to the water and was gone.

It was almost as hard saying good-bye a second time as it was the first, and of course I burst out crying. Suddenly I remembered something.

"Oh no, Reggie, I didn't ask her to meet me here again next year!" I looked out to sea, but of course, all I could see was waves. I called her and also used our two note code, but she didn't come back. That made me cry even harder. I felt like I had lost her all over again.

The sun was going down and Reggie's parents were calling us to go home. We headed back, me watching the ocean in case Mermary showed up again, though I knew she wouldn't. The Sea Kin were probably already far away by now.

In the car on the way back to Reggie's house, I remembered the ring she gave me. I took it out to look at it. It was a gold cameo ring, and the image was of a mermaid wrapped around a crescent moon!

"Reggie, look at the ring Mermary gave me!"

"Wow, that's cool! Her tail even kind of looks like the Lady of the Lake's tail. Her dress, I mean."

I hadn't noticed, but it did. The ring sort of reminded me of my dream the night before we set Mermary free. Somehow it made me feel a little better. It was too big for me to wear, but I knew it would fit me some day.

"Maybe she'll show up next year anyway," Reggie said. "We'll come back."

We did go back on the same day the following year, but Mermary didn't show up. After a few years, I didn't cry on the anniversary anymore.

As time went on I realized it was for the best. Mermary made that promise to me the first time not knowing what was ahead of her, before she learned the ways and needs of the Sea Kin. Mermary was with her people now, and that's where she needed to be. They had been very kind to allow her to come the first year, especially since they were so distrustful of humans. I had to accept that she probably wouldn't ever come back again.

As I got older, I realized that even though it had seemed like I was the one always teaching Mermary, I had been learning from her too. Not just about mermaids, but about responsibility and friendship, imagination and wisdom, kindness, love, and even ethics; lessons I would remember for the rest of my life.

And I did see her again, even if it was only in dreams. They were so real, I was sure Mermary must be sending them to me. I would be having a normal dream, when suddenly there would be water everywhere, and I knew Mermary was coming into my dream. I would run into the dream water and swim to her, and we would laugh and play the way I always wished I could do in real life. I thought of those dreams like the waves of two oceans that connected sometimes, which Mermary made happen so we could be together. It was magical.

So in a way, I didn't miss her at all. I knew she would always be with me.

Xequina is a storyteller, writer, artist and children's librarian. The inspiration for The Mermaid Girl came from the very first dream she had about a mermaid when she was five years old. Xequina is also a cartoonist, and draws and paints mermaids as well as many other magical and spiritual themes. She authored a column on Mexican spirituality, La Post Modern Curandera, for *The New Mission News* in San Francisco. She is currently working on another children's book, *The Witch Tree*, set in northern California. Xequina has degrees in Literature, Art, and Women's Spirituality. She lives in Oakland, California with her partner and their two bad cats.

Made in the USA
Lexington, KY
03 October 2018